REALM WALKER

Books in the Realm Walker Series
In the Shadows
The Land of Lost Souls
Hidden Passages
The Ring of Betrayal

Realm Walker Prequel
Heart of Darkness
Soul of Malice

Other Realm Walker Companion Books
The Origin: Marya's Journal
Soul Fire
Life After Death

Realm Walker World Books – coming soon!
Love at Frost Bite
Accidental Ghost: Soul Catcher Vol.1

Other Young Adults Series
The Bloodseekers
Zombie Girl
Hidden Journals
Baby Girl

MARSIDIA

Life after Death

Elle Klass

Life after Death

Copyright©2025 by Elle Klass
Published by Books by Elle, Inc.
ISBN: 978-1-951017-51-4
All rights reserved
Editor Dawn Lewis

Author's Disclaimer

1

ottles clank against each other in the cloth bag Sulien carries. A griffin snorts in the distance. Its sound distinct and ethereal. In the middle mountains the air is always chilly in the morning. All that defines day and night in Marsay is the temperature and moisture.

Above the fogline is cold and wet. The warlocks living high in the mountains use the clouds and moisture to their advantage. It is hard living. Those who live below the fogline, like Sulien, aren't as small community oriented and more political.

He places a large boot on the first wooden step. At nearly two and a half meters tall he isn't a small man. The second step groans under his weight, though he's not particularly heavy for his height. The last step protests as he raises his hand to knock.

The door swings open before his fist hits the wood. "You're just in time. I used my last on tea this morning."

Sulien lowers the cloth bag to the table and drops the handles. They fall against the sides of the bag revealing two large jars of sap. Sap is a great business for Sulien. The trees on his land overflow with it. Some has medicinal value, while others prevent the wear and tear of warlock aging, yet others assist with temperament. The flavors and uses aren't so much the trees as magic gifts granted to him by the source.

It is the sentient center of magic. All magic. He is a healer of sorts, but not always through conventional methods. Some of his gifts are better not spoken of. His customers don't know of his forbidden magic. Yet his magic, like all magic, is bequeathed to him through the source. It is the things not spoken of that others fear. Therefore he keeps his abilities to himself and customers keep their orders coming on a regular basis.

REALM WALKER

Magic has a balance to it. It isn't merely the runes the source provides. The marks linked to their abilities, carefully crafted skills imbued to each warlock.

Felan is a small woman. Her long golden hair braided with a ribbon that runs the length of her spine and eyes the color of amber. She is a beautiful woman. She invites him to sit down and enjoy a tea before his journey home. It isn't but a good thirty-minute journey on foot. He doesn't mind and often stays a few minutes when his customers request it.

Seran, her seven-year-old daughter, tugs at her mom's arm. Her golden curls bouncing with sad excitement. "Mommy." Her eyes bubbling in wetness.

Felan's eyes turn toward the child. "What is it?"

"The shrike I found. It's not moving. It's dead." Her tiny voice worried and torn with sadness.

Sulien stands and walks to the cage. The tiny animal sits on the bottom in the leaf clutter. Its feet tucked under its blue and green feathered body, eyes closed. "No dear, I'm sure it's only napping," he says and pushes a hand under his hair, pulling out a strand. Quietly, under his breath so the child and her mother can't hear, he utters to the small, feathery beaked animal: "Death isn't the end of your life. It is the beginning."

Life after Death

The animal fluffs its feathers as if waking from a slumber.

"It was napping!" the girl exclaims, joy pushing away the sadness.

Sulien smiles at the girl then turns to Felan. "It's time I leave. Thank you for the tea. Until next week."

She smiles, unsure exactly what he did or if he did anything, and bids him a good afternoon.

The midday air warms his skin. The source has given him the ability to bring life back from death in animals. It isn't a skill he shares with others. The villagers have their suspicions. So long as he provides them sap to fill their needs they don't talk.

It takes sacrifice for such strong magic to occur. It is *the* forbidden skill. Necromancy is feared in all of Marsay. In the case of the shrike, he used a plug of his hair. The sacrifice depends on the ask.

"The patient is almost recovered," Leif states as Sulien enters the lab beneath his home. The stone walls keep it cool, tools of his trade litter the long stone table where he cultivates the sap with spells and alchemy. Recently, he'd found a griffon with an injured foot and brought him home to the lab. A few days of healing sap and it is nearly ready to leave. It purrs as Sulien pets its soft head and rubs behind its ears.

Realm Walker

Leif runs a hand through his short, dirty blonde hair. "I don't think he wants to leave." The griffon brushes his head against Leif's hands urging him to pet him.

"We've made a lifelong friend," Sulien utters as he smooths the velvety fur of the griffon. Its plumose tail sweeps the worn stone floor, pushing dirt with it.

In the evening, the colorful lights pulse through the air and an evening chill swells through the open windows. Leif sets two plates at the table. He's been Sulien's assistant since he was orphaned. Sulien hadn't made it to his parents in time and they died. Leif was ten and had nowhere to go and Sulien needed an assistant. He'd trained him over the years and their relationship grew. Not only is it a working relationship and a good one but Sulien is a surrogate dad.

Sulien's brows furrow and he meets Leif's gaze as a knock on the door interrupts their meal of steaming broth loaded with vegetables and chunks of meat. The rich aroma of earthy spices filling their nostrils. Sulien closes his eyes and shakes his head as Leif pushes out his chair. The hefty wooden door opens with a creak.

Two sentries in navy uniforms with gold trimmed edges on the collar stand on the porch. Their posture straight and unwavering like ancient tree trunks. Their faces painted with stern looks. They lack any emotion or decency for interrupting the meal. *Do they go home to their families with the grim faces they always wear?*

As warrior warlocks they are chosen because of their speed, agility runes, strength, and cunning. Ones that make them good fighters. Once a year, during the trials, new sentries are chosen. All Marsay watches them fight one another with magic. It's frightening and mesmerizing as equally matched warriors duck and punch. Streams of magic billow from their hands fashioned into weapons of destruction. The most skilled, or those who survive, are chosen.

A rising thrum of voices mingles with marching feet rings in his ears. Sulien's heart sinks as he joins Leif at the door, studying the sentries and growing throng of townspeople. So many familiar faces sullen and angry. His heart breaks in two. These people are his clients. He's delivered them sap for all things over the years and now they look on him with horror in their eyes.

The shorter sentry, a female, meets his gaze. Her dark eyes studying his, her dark hair cropped above her ears. Runes peek out from the cloth on her neck. "Which of you is Sulien the sap maker?" Her unyielding frame matches her steely gaze.

REALM WALKER

2

Sulien's bushy, gray-speckled eyebrows drop as he narrows his eyes on the sentries. He has a soft, humble heart but his brain is logical and steady. He is a man of science as much as a compassionate healer. "I'm Sulien. What is this about?"

"You need to come with us," the female sentry states in her firm voice.

Hot stones pummel his heart, flames rise from its core. He's known on some level this day would come. A gray tunic covers his runes and the one that makes him different; feared. Letting out a slow breath, steadying himself, he responds, "You didn't answer my question."

The taller, bulkier sentry clears his throat while the smaller clicks a staff on the wooden deck of Sulien's porch as if to be sure Sulien has seen it and understands this isn't a friendly call. He stares into their eyes and whispers into Leif's ear. "Take care of things here until I return."

Leif steps to the side and turns to Sulien. A private conversation between their gazes as Leif's blue eyes turn as dark as the sentries' uniforms and a slow blink confirms he understands everything.

Sulien always feared the day may come when they'd burn him at the post, literally, for his practices. He's always taken great care to keep the parts that warlocks fear the most from their untrusting eyes.

As if the source itself is unhappy about the pitchfork routine, the air grows dark as the soft, colorful lights radiating from it cease. The last of the lights, high in the sky, disappear into the fog as Sulien marches with the sentries. The shorter one in front, the taller behind, and the townsfolk, absent of actual pitchforks, thrust light balls into the sky grumbling and blaming him. Their mutters claim the source is unhappy with him and that's why darkness fell, leaving the land in twilight.

Realm Walker

The dooming throng of the village walks with him and the sentries to the high court. The milky darkness of the room cuts with plasma bouncing in the tubes fast, hot, and white. Its light dances on the wooden slatted walls. The sentries close the doors behind them leaving him alone with his thoughts. He paces to and fro, hands folded behind his back, thoughts circling his head.

He has only delivered sap, having nothing else to do with the townsfolk. Surely the sap isn't the reason for his sudden captivity. Unaware of how much time passes, the door finally opens and the supreme regional wizard enters.

Her diadem, made with fine navy and silver-colored fabrics and precious metals, stands high on her head. Adorned in royal regalia in a navy-colored jacket trimmed in silver thread. A sentry drops a chair in the middle of the room and lifts the navy shoulder cape as the supreme wizard sits. Another sentry places a chair across from the wizard and motions for Sulien to sit.

Confused, disheartened, and curious as to what he could have done to be questioned by a warlock of such importance, he studies the wizard's face. Her thick eyebrows neatly groomed, unlike Sulien's that stick out at every angle. Her features chiseled with many fine wrinkles embedded in her brown skin as the regional wizard is never

Life after Death

young. Warlocks have long lives that cover many spans if they are lucky.

With her chin high and shoulders square, the regional wizard says, "It has come to my attention that you visited the home of Felan today. Is this true?"

New fire claims the ashen edges of his heart. The hot stones moving through his veins. The shrike. He'd saved it, a small sacrifice for a small animal. A simple hair from his thick mop. Showing no emotion, the anger and sadness welling within him will only give the regional wizard fodder for her accusations. Holding his head high and forcing emotions into an emptiness he responds. "Yes. I made a regular sap delivery."

"Was there a shrike found by the child?" His words steady and controlled as they meet the hard gaze of the wizard.

"Yes."

The regional wizard draws in a deep breath. Her expressionless face doesn't give anything away but her tone does. A hint of distrust mixed with alarm. "Did you bring the shrike back to life?"

Lying to the regional wizard is foolish, but more foolish is admitting to the practice of necromancy. He chooses his words carefully. "The bird was merely sleeping. I simply woke it."

Realm Walker

"Do not lie to me!" The regional wizard's voice rises and fills the space of the room with command.

His actions with the shrike small and subtle, he is sure Felan hadn't overheard him or seen the slight tug when he pulled a sprig of his hair. He makes a choice; lie or continue skirting the truth. Studying the harsh lines on the regional wizard's face he chooses to lie, as skirting the truth won't make the wizard less trusting of him nor will it solve the problem. Yet, why does anyone care about a simple shrike? "I have healing magic bestowed on me by the source, but I do not have abilities to bring back life from death. Explain what this is really about."

The wizard's face flashes in a rage before composing itself. She doesn't like being questioned. "You don't ask the questions. You answer."

Sulien's blood boils and he has a hard time not allowing his anger to distort his face. The hot stones flaming through his blood. Reining in his emotions, he responds: "Of course. I'm confused. Forgive me."

The regional wizard rolls her shoulder as the cape falls over her arm. "The young girl, Seran, has fallen gravely ill. The practice of necromancy takes one great sacrifice. Did you give the child's life to save the shrike?"

That was it. Sadness fills Sulien's heart that anyone could think he'd do such a thing.

Life after Death

A wave of remorse for the child and her family fills him to the brim, dousing the flaming hot stones. His tone soft: "Of course not. I would never, but if you take me to the child, I may be able to save her before it's too late."

"I will do no such thing." The wizard's face contorts as her shoulders billow backwards. "Necromancy has been banned in all of Marsay for centuries. The saving of a single life, no matter how small, can bring about an unfortunate series of events and many deaths. Do you, Sulien, practice necromancy?" Condemnation erupts in the wizard's words, wrapping Sulien in a cloak of judgment.

The air tense and strangling, Sulien stands, the chair falling behind him, crashing to the floor. His soul chokes on the distrust and fear.

It has been spans past, in ancient times, since a necromancer brought to life an army of the dead. Their bones protruding through the rotting skin of the century's dead animals. A conquest of power to overtake Marsay. She was highly revered until her quest for power. *Why? Why would she create something so beastly and raw if she hadn't been shunned in some way?*

The source trusted her with the magic it enshrined in him. Had they also grown weary and alarmed of magic they didn't understand and faulted her as they are him? Convicted without a trial, did she revolt against them?

Her death entombed in flames. Her army burning with her. Their ashes falling over the land. As if her ghost whispered in the air. Its cold tentacles wrapping Sulien in an icy chill that fills his words as if they are hers and not his own. "I do not and have done nothing wrong! Take me to the child so I may attempt to heal her."

The regional wizard waves a hand over her shoulder and the sentries hot foot it from the door; one lifting the wizard's cape as she stands. "Take him to the nook." Her voice bounces in anger as she turns, not giving Sulien another glance.

Life after Death

3

Leif, with the griffon he named Sisimo, meaning loyal friend, watches the parade into the center of town. The light balls giving enough glow they don't miss anything as they hide in the mountains under the fogline. It is a spectacle, and one he feared since the day Sulien revealed to him he is a necromancer. Anger and frustration bubble in his core. The warlocks fear what they don't understand.

Leif understands well that only the source can truly bring life from death. It is a rune, given to Sulien, one he protects and hides, one that has great power to heal the dead of infirmity, returning them firmly to the land of the living. Over the years, Leif learned the skills of healing and necromancy, yet hasn't earned the privilege of the rune yet. He hopes one day.

Of the runes he does have are excellent hearing. Invoking the rune, he listens to the sound waves rising in the air. Sulien wouldn't exchange a warlock life for that of a shrike.

Returning to the lab, he paces. Sisimo curled in the corner, his dark eyes following Leif's movements. "I don't understand." He rakes a hand through his dirty blonde hair and it drops back into its original resting position. His eyes focus on the floor in thought. "What can we do?" Sisimo stretches out his front paws and lays his beaked head on them.

It isn't the answer Leif wants. On the table are all types of remedies. Another of Sulien's runes grants him the ability to imbue magic into potions or sap, anything really. Leif doesn't have that rune either but understands alchemy well. Glass bottles and sprigs of jessup, ikatar, and other herbs lay on the table next to tinctures filled with various saps and other liquids. His eyes widen as an idea forms. "We can make a potion that will soften warlock abilities, long enough to rescue him from the nook!"

Life after Death

Sisimo shifts his head to the side, away from Leif, and gives a small growl. "If we put it in the water it can work." The griffon doesn't respond. Leif, defeated, drops into a chair. "Do you have a better idea?"

Sisimo snorts and stands, brushing past Leif as he makes his way to the steps. He cocks his head and side-glances him with a bird-like eye then lifts a front paw onto the first step.

Leif follows behind, understanding the griffon's actions mean sleep on it. He tosses and turns, Sisimo curls in the corner of the small room. Fluffing the pillow beneath his head he rolls to his left side then again to his right. He wishes he could sleep soundly like Sisimo. In the small kitchen is a collection of Sulien's magical saps, unwinding the top of the sleep potion he lets two drops fall onto his tongue. The sweet sap fills his mouth and drains down his throat, leaving a sugary aftertaste.

A few minutes later he is asleep. His and Sisimo's quiet snores in rhythm with each other. Leif's mind in utter darkness when a single dot of light flits and bounces followed by a voice. *It is time to leave. Marsay has taught you all you can learn. Your destiny is greater than any warlock can perceive.*

The dot of light spreads, revealing a red sky and golden rolling hills of sand. Cracks in the ground open up and fill with a viscous crimson liquid. *You have all the tools you need to find the desolate land. Follow your instincts. We won't be able to reach you once you have entered the middle realms, but the source will always be with you, Drakal.*

Leif jolts upright in bed as his eyes pop open. The visionaries. He'd heard of such messages. In the early days of history warlocks fled with visions of other lands. In numbers, they found their way out of Marsay to never return, making homes in realms Leif knows little of. In the mountains of Marsay is a small group of warlocks with eye runes. They watch life in other realms. It is a solemn destiny he thinks. Lonely and solitary, and considers himself lucky he isn't granted such a rune.

His mind reels to the implications of the vision and the name Drakal. In warlock, it means death keeper. He doesn't save life or challenge death. The name is more suited for Sulien, not him, yet they called him Drakal. Surely, it is a mistake.

The desolate land appeared harsh, unlivable. What is he to do in that place? *Follow his instincts.* In that moment, they told him to save Sulien. '*You have all the tools you need*' bounces and bobbles in his head. His ability to hear, Sisimo, his loyal friend thinks '*plasma*'... He lifts his shirt, eyes wandering to another room. He runs a finger over a black splatter in the shape of a gust of wind and another with the warlock word for conceal.

𝕷𝖎𝖋𝖊 𝖆𝖋𝖙𝖊𝖗 𝕯𝖊𝖆𝖙𝖍

One allows him to move the air. It hides him from others. The source gave them with intent. The rune didn't seem to have a purpose, he begins to understand. *Intent*.

4

etal slats above his head would have allowed the rainbow of soft light in if there was any. No doubt the warlocks blame him for the source's anger, but it isn't him. The girl fell ill because she fell ill, possibly in her rescue of the shrike she collected whatever illness the bird carried.

The nook is several feet deep with smooth dirt walls. He sits on the rocky dirt floor, knees to his chest, arms folded over them in thought. The air underground is always moist, with a steady temperature. He has no idea how much time has passed. His mind floats on the idea of escape. Surely Leif is aware of his circumstances.

If escape is possible, where will they go? The idea of finding the middle realms clings to the edge of his subconscious. He lays his head against the smooth dirt wall and closes his eyes. His mind fills with visions of a land flowing with a crimson, snaking river and cracked golden sand. Every time he closes his eyes he sees it. The same forsaken land. Not a single scaled, fuzzy, or shelled animal peeks in and out of the cracks in the ground or runs over the dehydrated soil. There are no trees or flowers. It is a barren place, not suitable for anything.

No matter how much he dismisses the idea, the land is all he sees when his eyelids drop. The place becomes comfortable. Running his hand over the smooth dirt floor he whispers, "What is it you want me to do?"

Go there… The words carry through the still air of the nook.

This is your destiny. I will show you the way. The words bounce in his head as his eyes pop open. *You will find the barren land flowing in blood in the middle realms.*

The voice comes from all around, it echoes through the nook. "Who are you?" he asks.

REALM WALKER

I am like you, was like you. Find the desolate land and use your rune to make a people. A strong people who won't bend to the warlocks. Who thrive on the only resource — blood.

He considers the voice isn't real. It's a figment of his imagination. He's been trapped in the nook too long and insanity is sneaking in on him.

"How do I find these realms and the desolate land?"

The voice doesn't come. His words lost in the persistent silence. He repeats them.

The voice returns with one last statement that floats through the air as a whisper: *Leif will guide you.*

This isn't from the visionaries. It is something different. Its energy fuzzy and prickly. A dark shadow catches the corner of his eye. When he turns his head, the room is empty.

The middle realms are lands filled with strange beings. Ones who long ago departed from Marsay, no longer warlock but something else. The stories surrounding the realms are filled with horrors of tainted magic and impish, hateful creatures.

The dream showed him something different. The unfamiliar voice challenging him, egging on a destiny of creating a creature suited for a harsh environment. A place to practice necromancy; to bring life back from death. The idea grows and forms before the metal grate opens and a rope ladder swings down for him to climb.

His hands tied in metal rope behind his back, he walks peacefully to the middle of the town where the pyre awaits. Is he to be burned without a fair trial? To become ash on the land as the last necromancer? Was the vision false, his mind playing tricks?

The townsfolk circle the pyre like scavenging predators, screaming hateful words at him, calling him a murderer. A few refuse to look upon him as if guilt riddles their hearts, or maybe sorrow. Surely some support him, but will any be brave enough to speak out for him? Their shoulders hunched and heads turned in shame, they won't. Flames will consume him.

His heart sinks at the thought of the sweet child dead, especially when he could have saved her. Maybe she's not dead and he can still save her. His heart deflates. The regional wizard won't allow it, remembering her ugly words. His back to the pyre, sentries tie him to it. The metal ropes around him subdue the plasma magic every warlock contains as their first rune. It is a simple lightning bolt.

The regional wizard, with a sentry on each side, steps forward. Her expression as inflexible as the night she took him from his home. The crowd swallows their words, creating a pervasive silence that rattles Sulien to the core. "Do you, Sulien, practice necromancy?"

His eyes adjust to the twilight, a place somewhere between true darkness and light, they are forced into a squint when plasma beams are thrust into the sky creating temporary light. A dark shadow covers the ground from the mountains and direction of his home. He dares not look in its direction but allows his eyes to study the shape in its shadow form. A long tail acts as a rudder, swooshing in a circular pattern. His heart lifts but his eyes remain trained on the ground, watching the shadow grow closer.

The regional wizard repeats herself in her unyielding tone, as if she alone has the authority to denounce him or challenge the source. It is the true judge and jury and gives magic based on the strength of each warlock. He has the necromancer's mark for a reason and now he understands his fate. Through the dream, the source spoke directly to him and showed him the path, he thinks.

The regional wizard raises her arm, calling on a sentry to light a torch. Fire erupts at the sentries' fingertips, wrapping around the wick of the torch. Flames burn steadily. The plasma lights of the townspeople simmer into nothingness, allowing the flames to light the air as they lick at its oxygen. The regional wizard asks one more time, "Do you, Sulien, practice necromancy?" Her voice carries.

Life after Death

The shadow high and close, nearly above him, Sulien raises his eyes and meets the regional wizard's dark eyes and furrowed brows. "I merely woke a sleeping bird." With laser precision, a plasma beam extends from the sky and cuts across the metal ropes binding Sulien's hands and magic.

They hit the ground with a thud. He claps his palms, enacting an elemental rune he's rarely had use for. The earth rumbles under the feet of the regional wizard, who sways as she attempts to steady herself. Air cuts above Sulien and swishes as talons clutch his shoulders.

The regional wizard's voice booms: "Light the pyre, light the air with plasma."

Flames lick the wood and straw as Sulien drifts above it. Talons pierce the cloth of his cloak and rest against the flesh of his shoulders. His feet and legs saturated in heat. Below, a sea of faces gawks upwards. Smoke eddies around them as the fire consumes the wood of the pyre.

A single blue plasma beam cuts through the darkness and haze twists around his legs. The griffon's wings push against it as the animal scrambles to get higher. The plasma tugs at his legs, a tendril climbing to his waist. The tips of the griffon's talons dig under his arms like tiny prickling needles and smoke rises from the pyre.

Realm Walker

Something darker than twilight tumbles end over end, its sharp point slicing through the plasma beam, taking a sliver off the sole of his shoe. A strong wind eddies the smoke and pushes it towards the warlocks on the ground, engulfing them. The plasma tendril extends over his middle, evaporating as the griffon finally gets traction thanks to the wind and lifts them high into the air.

The faces below lose detail through the smoke and distance until they are tiny, obscure dots, and vanish when the fogline welcomes them.

On the other side, in the darkness of twilight, the griffon lowers and lets go of Sulien, who drops twenty or so centimeters. His toasted feet burning as they catch him. The animal folds his wings over his back after his landing and he pushes his head against Sulien's chest. Sulien pulls a hand through the animal's fur and leans his head against the griffon's. Its softness gives Sulien a feeling of safety.

Leaves and small crunches alert Sulien, his head rising and eyes darting toward the noise. Through the fog, a form moves towards him. Lanky and tall, he recognizes Leif who greets him with a quirky smile of satisfaction.

They don't have long before the regional wizard will send sentries their way, but they'll have to ask permission from the local regional wizard. The source with them and willing, they have a day to escape Marsay.

The mountains above the fogline are filled with caves. Crystals embedded in the walls hum with light as they enter. It is as if the source offers a blessing. Sulien paces as Leif leans against the wall.

"We must leave Marsay forever. I was shown a vision of a land we must find. It is my destiny and yours. A place we can create a people who will make use of a desolate land. A people who will gain a second chance at life."

Leif raises an eyebrow in question. A trick Sulien can't do. If one of his bushy eyebrows rises, the other soon follows. "I too heard the voice and the visionaries showed me a vision. Our destiny ends in the desolate land flowing in crimson. Sisimo is strong. He can carry us into the clouds and through the veil into the middle realms."

Goosepimples work their way over Sulien's skin. He's seen the land too. The unfriendly, sterile land flowing in blood. The crimson liquid of life. "What else did the visionaries show you?"

"Nothing," he is quick to respond, "but once we leave Marsay they won't be able to communicate. It is up to us to use our runes to find the land. The source has granted us all we need."

Realm Walker

Since when did Leif get so philosophical and wise? It happened in a blink under his nose. The boy is no longer a child. He is a man and this vision is his as much as Sulien's, maybe it is more Leif's than Sulien's. He is not convinced it was the source who spoke to him in the nook. The shadow in the corner of his eye, in the darkness of the hole in the ground, lingers. A female voice spoke and a shadow formed in his peripheral.

The griffon curls on the rocky floor, a warm stream of air escaping his mouth as he rests. "We must go to the middle realms." No warlock will follow them into the realms for their fear of the nomadic creatures with twisted magic they call realm walkers.

5

Air rushes over Leif's head and back as they rise into the sky, above the trees and through the fog. Sisimo took a long nap while they conjured food. All they have to do is think of what they want and turn a branch into an entire feast, one that includes something for griffons too.

Drops of humidity tickle his skin on the ascent. Once through the veil, water surrounds him, not in a cocoon of safety, but a lake or spring. A ball of light dances along the surface as his weightless body floats towards it. No longer on Sisimo's back, his eyes roam the liquid surroundings for his tail or a wing, anything to tell him he is close.

Ripples shatter the glassy surface, moving the reflection of the light ball into jagged, twisted lines, and his ears fill with a large splashing sound as if someone has jumped into a fjord. Marsay has many, as so many of the waterfalls drop into long valleys before falling into another.

When the water settles, his head bobs through the surface. Twisting it, he spots Sisimo sitting on his haunches at the edge of the body of water. The salt and pepper head of Sulien jogs above the surface as he swims towards the shore.

Large, yellow, five petal blooms trimmed in gold eddy in and out as Leif treads water. Above him are thick branches filled with silver leaves larger than his hand. Roots brush and wrap his ankles and against his legs, propelling him towards the shore as if his presence isn't wanted. Ducking his head beneath the surface, balls of gold shimmer over the water's sandy basin with no sign of the veil they emerged through.

He grabs at a gold ball, watery sand falls through his fingers. He extends them and captures as many gold balls as will fill his hand and stuffs them into a pocket in his trousers. Running a hand over the surface of the water, he catches two flowers and a handful of leaves

Life after Death

at the edge of the water as the roots unwrap from his legs, depositing him at the shore.

The tree, mountainous in size, stands erect in the middle of the moat they came through. The Serenity Tree. Having never seen it, every warlock knows it connects to the source. Its roots extend into the cavern no warlock dares enter, where the source radiates magic and light. It provides life, without it there would be nothing, a lifeless void.

Its seeds are said to hold the secret of immortality. No warlock has seen much less tested the idea. At the least its flowers and leaves must hold medicinal value and, as an apprentice to a necromancer, seem an important thing to save.

A wet hand rests on Leif's as he scoops the leaves and flowers into a satchel. "You shouldn't take those." Sulien states.

He continues carefully dropping the mix into the satchel, not ignoring Sulien per se. "There will never be another chance. The possible medicinal value makes it worth the while."

Warlocks are all types of superstitious. Stories passed from one generation to the next coalesce as Sulien states his next words: "Having those in your possession could doom us. No one person is allowed to hold life and immortality in their hands, not even a necromancer. I can only grant what the source has allowed me. Those flowers and petals are the essence of life. Their magic is more powerful than anything we've ever witnessed."

That is the purpose. If they are to create life in a desolate, barren land then they need something powerful, something containing the essence of life. The visionaries told him to follow his instincts and that's precisely what he's doing. "We aren't in Marsay anymore, magic is weak here, can't you feel it? These may be what we need to bring life back from death."

Sulien's wide mouth curls into a smile of sorts. "Maybe you are right." He pulls his hand away. "This land is very different than home."

The sky dark with a silver ball of light. Its soft glow shadows the landscape and tiny sparkles of light twinkle in and out. There are no horizontal streams of rainbow light that spill upwards from the source and the air doesn't drip in magic so thick it is syrupy. The air is thinner. Dense croppings of trees don't shine in bioluminescence, but small blue flowers do. Their petals glow cyan at the bases of trees. It is pretty, a different pretty than Marsay.

Sisimo stretches under the wide branches of a tree and lays his head over his front paws. No doubt he needs a rest, carrying them into the air and through the veil was an exertion, but in a few hours he'll be ready to go.

Sulien picks a few flower petals from the ground and stares at them for a minute before making a profound statement: "We can't conjure food and I don't know what is safe to eat in its raw form."

Leif picks a handful of blue glowing flowers, stuffing them into his satchel. "I brought a few things in case we needed them. They are in the large satchel wrapped around Sisimo's belly." He prepared. Although the food is surely soaked, it will still be edible, just mushy.

Leif settles against the thick base of a tree as Sisimo eats the wet nuts Sulien places before him. He needs to regain his energy before they head anywhere. If either of them know where to go. In his gut, Leif isn't worried. He stretches his feet to get comfortable. Sulien leans against the wide trunk of a tree across from him, a solemn expression marring his face.

"After a good rest we will figure out which way to go," Leif states matter-of-factly. As far as he can see in the silvery bathed twilight, are trees and delicate glowing blue flowers. Peace rests in his heart as he closes his eyes.

Sulien harumphs, not seeming so sure they'd figure out how to get to the desolate, barren wasteland.

Realm Walker

A bright light forces Leif's eyes open after a long sleep not filled with visions or dreams. Bands of yellow filter through the purple and green leaves of the trees. The silvery ball in the sky replaced with one that radiates golden light and the blue flowers no longer glow. Their flowers closed.

He opens the satchel and the ones he'd saved still glow in bioluminescent glory. Tightening the bag, he doesn't want them to stop and wonders how long they'll continue glowing in the darkness of the bag. The ground is covered in a soft, silvery grass and an array of color pops up as tiny flowers in purple, gold, red, and pink sway with a cold breeze. He shudders under his cloak from the chill. The realm doesn't lack any color, nor did Marsay, but it is *different*.

The word tarries on his brain as rustling leaves catch the attention of his ears. Turning on his supersonic hearing, the rhythmic palpitations of a heartbeat carry through his brain. Shifting his eyes in the direction of the sound, they see no animals, only plants. Do they have heartbeats? In this new realm, he understands nothing of it. Plants could possibly walk and talk here, have multichambered hearts even.

The Serenity Tree is more glorious in the light. Its silver leaves shine under the golden light. Sisimo stirs and tilts his beaked head towards Leif. "It is beautiful, isn't it? Don't worry we'll find the way."

Sisimo ruffles his fur in the chilly air. Marsay stays one temperature and is warmer than this place. He hadn't noticed the cold the previous night, perhaps it was the excitement. Digging into the large satchel with food he brings out more nuts for Sisimo and berries for himself.

They are dry now. The sweetness of the skin bursts in his mouth followed by the sour insides. The mixture tingles as he swallows them. He chose the gwash for its protein, carbohydrates, and flavor. One of the few fruits in Marsay that is an entire meal.

A wave of silvery grass brushes past Leif as Sulien sits upright, having fallen to the ground in his sleep. A hand over his eyes to shield the light from the bright orb in the sky, he peers upwards. "A light for darkness and a brighter one for…day."

Leif is sure Sulien knows more of these realms than he does but isn't sure how much. "Do you know which realm we are in?"

Sulien's large mouth twitches at the corners, his eyes on the Serenity Tree as if mesmerized by the orbs of light shining on the silver leaves. "I think it's called Aradia, but I don't know how we get to the desolate land from here."

Leif has no answer. Aradia. His mind toys with the word.

Realm Walker

Sulien jumps to his feet as if stung by a thumper, a tiny insect with a stinger as long as it's body. They make for good syringes but whop a heck of a sting. His feet crunch on dry ground as the grass appears to move out of the way of his boots. It's a curious thing.

Sulien's large shoulders round as he lowers himself onto his knees, arms stretched in front of him. "Did you bring needles?" he calls.

Knowing better than to enter a foreign realm unprepared, Leif packed the large satchel appropriately. The inside pocket contains medicinal supplies. He fetches a thumper needle. Kneeling in the grass that parts for his knees, he spots a small, lifeless animal. Its tiny ears forming a rounded cone with fuzzy dark fur, a long pink nose on its face, and its body about the size as a ferret. Ferrets are sacred animals in Marsay. The animal is the most still thing he's seen since arriving in Aradia.

Sulien pokes his finger, a drop of blood bounces onto the head of the little animal as he chants, "Death isn't the end of your life. It is the beginning." No sooner does the last word leave Sulien's lips than the animal jumps to its feet, sniffs its pink nose at Sulien, and bounces away on its long hind legs.

Life after Death

"The magic isn't as strong here. It takes a blood sacrifice," Sulien says as he lifts his large frame onto his feet.

Leif opens his mouth to speak when he hears something different. His ears listening, the steady heartbeat returns.

"How did you do that?" a voice speaks in a commanding tone. It belongs to a small person with long dark hair tied into a braid hanging over her chest and dropping to her waist, a bow in her hands with a poised arrow. Purple and pink fluff standing on end as if in exclamation behind her. Bright brown eyes focus on Sulien as she steps over a fluffy colorful bush that parts in the middle to make room for her to step over it.

She doesn't look menacing, but the arrow pointed at Sulien's heart does.

REALM WALKER

6

Sulien doesn't appear threatened by the short woman or the arrow. His face melts into a soft, thoughtful expression as he contemplates lying or telling the short, long-haired young woman the truth. He puts both arms out to show he has no weapons, then brings his right arm over his chest and grabs hold of the edge of the brown cloak, bringing it over his arm. He pushes it onto his back then rolls up the sleeve of his shirt.

A black rune in the shape of a horizontal 8 rests on his bicep. The young woman narrows her gaze on his arm, her arrow steady and aimed at his chest. "We are warlocks and come from a realm hidden from your eyes. This mark gives me an ability to salvage life in the twilight of death."

Twisting her lips, she considers her words, a cool breeze pushes stray strands of hair over her cheeks, lips, and nose. Pulling the bowstring back, she asks, "Why would you tell me this?" Her tone cross examining. Unsure whether she should trust him or not.

"Because we have an important job and need your help."

Leif stands still, watching and listening to the conversation, ready to blow the arrow in a different direction should she let it fly.

Releasing the tension on the bow, she lowers the weapon. "You desecrate the Serenity Tree then bring a dead muchuchka to life and you want me to help you. It seems you *think* you can do anything you want." The words fly from her mouth in a spray of spit.

"We have no intention of desecrating the Serenity Tree – issuer and keeper of life – but we have an important mission, one we have been sent here to accomplish and you seem quite capable of assisting us with a small task."

Her cheeks flush from the crisp, chilly air and she sucks in a deep breath and releases. Tiny drops of breath suspended in the air. "I'm not sure I want to help you or should. Really, I should turn you in but…if my assistance will get you out of my realm then I might consider it."

Sulien's wide lips almost curl into a smile as he quickly catches it and draws them back into a line. "Your help most certainly will. We must find the desolate wasteland."

Her eyes pop as she chokes on swallowed spit. "That place is dead, it flows in blood, it isn't habitable and ishostile. Why would you go there?"

Leif speaks, "It is habitable, not by any mortal being in any realm but a new life, one suited for its harsh lands."

As if noticing Leif for the first time, she turns her eyes on him. A full foot and a half taller than her he isn't as massive as Sulien and carries a slender, muscled build. The curls in his hair standing at various angles and his blue eyes mix in color. They meet hers for a second before her gaze travels down his body, taking in his gray cloak, trousers, and boots. "I think you are both unwell in the head…I can't ignore you aren't like any being I've ever met."

She steps to the side and walks around the men, then shifts her gaze to Sisimo. "You are larger than any being in the lower realms and nearly as large as anything from the highlands, yet not as bulky as a dragon and your eyes are not those of a harvester…and that creature of yours is part bird, part something else…You call yourself a warlock. I have no choice but to believe you and your bizarre ideas. You bring back life using a drop of blood. Is that your plan?"

"Something like that. It hasn't yet been revealed, but we must get to the desolate land," Sulien reiterates.

She drops to one panted knee, lays down her weapon, and draws in a naked slice of dirt not covered in silvery grass. "If you don't come closer you won't see."

The men join her, dropping a knee across from her in the grass and dirt. She draws triangles resembling mountains and a line going over them to a low-lying area. "If you can make it over the lava flows with that winged animal of yours you will get to the highlands. The journey through them will take you through to the desolate land but you must face the brutal dragons in Sier. Should you make it past them you will face the harvesters, as a necromancer you go against their beliefs and sole purpose. They send the souls of the dead to the afterlife." She lifts her attention from the dirt, setting her eyes squarely on Sulien who meets her gaze but doesn't respond, sensing she has more to say.

She draws another line, a half circle like the other. "There is an Aradian transport ship leaving tomorrow. It will sail through the lavender seas of Navarin." She pokes at the ground. "You and your animal must stay in the cargo hold and will need strong magic as the sylphs will likely find and kill you. They rule the land with an iron grip tighter than the dragon king of Sier. If you should make is safely over the lavender seas to Verboten the trolls will allow you to pass through their land, but it will cost."

"What will they accept as payment?" Sulien inquires, unsure what exactly Leif packed, but knowing if trees and sap or water exist in the land he can spell them into a potion, such as he did for the warlocks.

"Something of magical quality not easily found in any realm…There is one other way," she states as she draws a line straight from where they stand meeting the other two lines. "You can go straight through the treacherous lands, a place filled with swamps and serpents, jagged rocks, and other beings unwelcome in any realm. It is the most direct route."

Sulien doesn't think long. Leif has the cloaking rune and can hide them if needed from the sylphs as she called them. "I think we should like to take the transport ship."

Leif immediately baulks. "We should talk about this."

Agreeing, they walk several paces away from the young woman.

"The treacherous lands are the most direct route. The dangers don't seem any worse than the alternatives and we have magic given to us by the source for this mission. In my vision I was told I have everything I need to get to the desolate land and I should follow my instincts. They say we should head straight. Whatever dangers we face, we will conquer."

Leif's words impress Sulien. He's always made the decisions since Leif was a boy. He taught him all he knows, cared for him, raised him, and now he needs to trust in the young man who is no longer a boy. Placing a large hand on Leif's right shoulder, he allows a proud smile. "We shall do it your way."

REALM WALKER

7

Humid and smelling of everything rotten, the chartreuse water in the swamps bubble below Leif's feet as he steps from one stone to the next. Water splashes a few feet from him as something long and slender dives below the surface. The treacherous lands aren't pretty and are filled with unimaginable dangers as they'd flown over the sinking sands on rubbery vines hanging from tall trees whose roots are buried in the liquid sand.

The young woman, an elf named Libitina. Libby for short, insisted on being their guide. Claiming they wouldn't make it through without someone who knew the land. Her braid bounces as she hops gracefully from one slick stone to the next, spots of sticky deep purple moss grabbing the soles of her feet.

Water in the air clings to Leif's neck and clothing. Sulien insists on going last while Sisimo flies elegantly above them. His wings spread as he soars and flaps sending a breeze over Leif's head, cooling him through the water droplets on it. How the air went from cool in the beautiful land of Aradia to humid and sticky in the treacherous lands only a couple hours journey he doesn't understand.

The golden sky turning into bands of purple and pink as the great shiny orb falls over the horizon. Libby shouts as she hops to the next stone, bubbles splashing over it, "We are almost to the jagged stones. Take a short hop onto the glass sand and stop."

Two more hops and she halts, side-stepping carefully along a clear shelf she waits. Leif makes the hop next to her. The clear shelf more slippery than the stones but not as sticky as the moss. He nearly drops forward onto a bed of stones as pointed as any sword or arrow. Using the wind, he pushes himself upright and side-steps a couple feet next to her.

Sulien, tall enough, his long legs nearly take one large step from the last stone to the clear shelf. Sisimo drops low, his wings flapping gently in the wet air.

"The path is slippery and the sun is setting. Follow my steps exactly and we'll make it to the brass forest where we can camp for the night," Libby states, pointing towards something on the horizon not visible from Leif's vantage point. The clear shelf beneath him reflects the colors of the sky, repeated in the clear jagged rocks.

The path narrow, there is barely enough room for his boots that nearly get him stuck more than once. Her nimble tiny feet seem made for such a slender passage. When serrated rocks cover the path, she takes a step to the right then forward and to the left. He follows, watching each of her steps and mimicking them.

The shades of color in the sky are swallowed by near darkness. The shiny lights they'd seen when they first arrived dot the sky twinkling against the rocks and fragments. The glowing ball returns with the lights. It isn't silver anymore, but azure.

Ahead of them, the rocks thin and trees with shiny metallic trunks jut from the dark ground absent of reflection from above. One last step and the rocks clear. Soft patches of some type of grass grow thicker around the trees as they follow her into the brass forest. The air grows less wet and Sisimo, on foot now, stays close to Leif and Sulien.

Life after Death

Libby halts, swings her arms out and drops them behind her back, cupping her delicate hands. She turns on her heel. "We can camp here."

The grass, soft as silk, makes a nice bed as Leif rests his head against Sisimo's side. His beak nearly touches Leif's arm. The wispy leaves of the brass trees make for a sweet and salty meal. His eyes fall on Libby who snuggles on a patch of the silky grass, her small chest lightly rising and falling with each breath. Her long braid falling over the dirt. Tiny red lights blink open around her, surrounding her in a soft red glow.

Leif leans forward, a chill hitting his back as it leaves the side of the warm-blooded sleeping griffon. More tiny red lights blink on, blanketing all of them in a soft red glow. Crawling forward on his hands and knees, he studies the red lights. It is a tiny plant, the flower no bigger than his pinky nail and shaped like a heart. With pointer finger and thumb, he pulls the fragile plant from the ground and sets it in his palm, roots and all, eight tiny heart flowers glow crimson.

"Pretty aren't they?" Libby's sweet voice sails through the air.

"They are."

"They are the rarest of all realm flowers and are only found here." Libby, careful not to step on any of the tiny red dots, walks to him and sits cross legged.

46

REALM WALKER

"What do they do?"

Her eyebrows arch as if confused by his question. He restates, "Do they have medicinal value?"

Her lips curl into a smile. "No one knows. They are rare and not many come to the treacherous lands. Not many know the way as I do. I've been traveling between Aradia and Verboten since I was a child. Born in Verboten, my father is a troll and my mother an elvarin-elf who escaped to the treacherous lands as a child, unwanted because of her "unclean" blood. She taught me everything I show you of these lands. She did not tell me if the iolida has any medicinal value."

His heart warms to hear her speak of her family. They'd known each other less than a day and their trust is growing. "I was born of another realm, so different than this. Magic there is breathable, palpable in the air. My parents died when I was a child, born to them very late in life. Sulien took me in, taught me many things, like the beauty in plants and tree sap."

She folds his fingers over the tiny plant in the palm of his hand. "Keep it safe."

Her warm hand over his sending a ripple through him. When she lifts her hands the air feels chilly over his fingers. With a nod, he places the delicate red heart-shaped flowers in his satchel with the other plants he's collected. A rustle of leaves over his head catches his attention. He turns, coming face to face with two large fangs and a forked tongue sliding across his cheek leaving a trail of slime.

8

eif freezes as the animal's eye stares into his, deep and dark. Its gaze seems endless. His mind begs him to run but his feet refuse to move as if glued to the ground. An acrid odor wafts up his nostrils but the muscles in his face are as frozen as his feet and keep the grimace from sprouting.

From the corner of his eyes, a shadow moves, and something drops, pulling the one-eyed, fanged serpent downward. Instantly, his body unfreezes, and he swivels to watch a dark creature no more than a foot tall with a wide mouth sink a collection of pointed fanged teeth as sharp as clear jagged rocks into the serpent.

Its head drops, absent of its body. It slowly uncoils from a shiny branch and drops in a puddle near its decapitated head. The dark creature with its massive mouth munches on the serpent like it is dinner.

He jumps backwards and stumbles a few steps as laughter fills his ears. Turning, he watches Libby chuckle so hard her body rocks and glows yellow. Forgetting all about the serpent and creature gulping away he blinks and stammers, "You…you're glow…ing."

Libby's laughter halts, her brown eyes shift and her face turns a subtle pink like the feathers in her tail. She folds her arms over her chest. "This happens every time." Within a few seconds the glow dissipates. She doesn't offer more of an explanation, turning her attention to the rabid small beast who swallowed the last bite of serpent.

"Arley. I think you scared my client," Libby says as she joins Leif and the thirty or so centimeter tall dark creature.

It turns its dark eyes on Leif. Its skin leathery and head bald except for a few strands of hair visible under the twinkling sky. "Eat serpent. Delicious." It rubs its belly. Its wide mouth set in a toothy smile.

"I'm guessing you don't have dark nymphs wherever you come from. Serpents are their main food source. Don't worry, they have no interest in you," Libby says.

No, they didn't have dark nymphs in Marsay. They have ferrets, manticores that protect the source, griffons, Pegasus, a few types of birds and insects. "What was that serpent?"

"One that traps their prey by mesmerizing them then sinks their fangs in. The poison slowly paralyses the prey, turning its muscles to mush as its jaw unlatches, opens wide and gulps their prey in one swallow," Libby states, making a slurpy sound.

"Arley is here, you are safe from serpents," the dark nymph responds before Leif can ask any more questions.

Leif has a difficult time falling asleep after the incident. His eyes playing tricks as they watch for serpents, nymphs, or anything else that might live in the treacherous lands. Libby doesn't seem bothered as light snores escape her lips and Arley curls on a swatch of silky grass. Sisimo and Sulien slept through the entire ordeal.

His attention turns. The situation earlier familiar and he suddenly remembers he experienced it in a dream. He sits up, eyes to the starry sky, and thinks maybe it was a message telling him they are going in the right direction.

Life after Death

The brass forest gives way to what Libby calls the lake of faces. She warns them to stay on the walking bridge and stare ahead. If one looks into the water and sees the faces of the dead fae-hybrids they will disintegrate on the spot into dust. Their pieces blowing west to Navarin as fairy dust.

Waist-high green reeds with fluffy pink tails surround the lake. The bright sky orb Libby calls the sun reflects against the glassy surface of the water. Sisimo flies over the lake of faces and waits for them behind the fluffy pink tails on the other side. The lake is wider than it is long and the wooden bridge nothing more than a broad tree trunk.

Following behind the group, Arley stays close to Sulien, his stench making breathing nearly unbearable. Leif and Libby walk close and Sulien is glad to see a friendship growing between them. He is no longer the necromancer's apprentice, whispers in hushed tones, and is in his own right a man. The source's intentions for him unclear but certain, as the visionaries spoke to him, showed him more than Sulien. It is his turn to take the lead.

The bridge stays steady as Libby strides across it with ease and bounces off as she comes to the other side of the lake. Leif steps on, arms out for balance and scoots more than steps, the large satchel slips off his shoulder and nearly plummets into the water. He catches it in time but the movement knocks him off balance and he bobs, losing the satchel.

"Don't!" Sulien screams. Leif is more important for this mission so he jumps off, water splashing up to his armpits as he feels along the lake bottom with his boot. Leif's head turns. "No, go, get to the other side," he screams and dives under.

The bottom of the lake is replaced by a large woman with flowing silver hair. Her face a paper mache of wrinkles and eyes beams of light. "You must go in to find it."

Sulien swallows, his eyes doing everything to look away from her and find the satchel. Everywhere he glances, the woman with light beam eyes is there. He can't see anything else. He is done for, yet he hasn't disintegrated into fairy dust. She lifts a withered hand and pushes against his chest.

The old woman's face is replaced by many. They stare with open mouths and large eyes. Their hair flowing with the water. Sulien blinks his eyes to push them away. The satchel. Where is the satchel? Screams filter through the water, piercing his ears. He pushes his hands to his ears to force them out and something hits his back.

Life after Death

Pulling his hands from his ears he feels behind him. It is long, soft, yet lightweight and stiff. Ignoring the faces, he brings it in front of his eyes. A branch. Through the translucent faces, mouths gaping, eyes wide and fearful, is the satchel's strap.

He pushes the branch forward. Catching the strap, he tugs it towards him.

His lungs long for air to breathe as he clutches the satchel and stands, water falling from his long salt and pepper hair, ripples spreading over the mirrored surface.

"Sulien," a voice cries as something grabs under his arm pits and lifts him into the air, dropping him on the other side of the lake. He coughs and chokes as he stares at the foursome gazing down at him.

"You're not dust!" Leif exclaims as he drapes himself over Sulien.

All the years he raised him from boy to man he's never given him a hug, until today. Pushing a thick wet arm around Leif's back he revels in the moment. What it must feel like to have the love of a child. "Of course not. I'm tougher than the lake."

REALM WALKER

9

The few springs of hair bob above the rainbow of flowers as Arley climbs flora-covered rock shouting, "All the realms, all the realms." A leathery serpent pelt covers his little body.

Leif's long stride carries him to the top. He stands alongside Libby.

"That's where we started," she points. Dense trees provide a canopy over the land and, to the left, black ground that moves. Red splotches of molten rock bubble over the surface, the lava flows Libby told them about, and further to the right snow-capped mountains, winged creatures soaring over the top. He's glad they hadn't chosen that route. Surely they would have been dinner. To the west, circular lower highlands, covered in greenery and, finally, desert.

As far as the eye can see is golden sand and a red river snaking through it. He's reminded of his vision. A river that flows in blood. Of all the strange creatures that live in the treacherous lands what can possibly live in a land whose only sign of life is the blood that covers it?

Sulien joins them, hands resting on a cane fashioned from a weathered driftwood branch. Libby claims the wood of a fallen tree has magic value. It is the bridge between life and death.

"Blood Falls, it separates the mountains from the desert. It is the blood of all who die and pass to another life."

Sulien's nose twitches as if deep in thought, attempting to solve the unsolvable question that tarries on Leif's mind. The visionaries' words were clear. They had everything they needed and would find the solution.

Libby brushes chunks of hair fallen from her messy braid away from her face. Knowing her for only three days, it surprises him how much his heart aches at the idea of leaving her. Even Arley has grown on him, with the exception of his deathly stench.

Realm Walker

"Go straight and you'll enter the desolate wasteland, but look past it and you'll find the metal-gemstone forests of Verboten and the lavender seas of Navarin." The realms are mystifying and amazing, every bit as beautiful as Marsay. Leif sits down and stretches his legs as the sun lowers on the horizon.

The smells of whatever plant they are cooking makes his stomach rumble. This might be the last good meal he'll have, yet he can't take his eyes off the wasteland. *How?* he questions. *Intent* carries on the wind. He closes his eyes, trying to picture a life in that land that isn't filled with famine.

"I thought you might be hungry," Libby says as she hands him a leaf filled with some type of fleshy plant dish. Lowering herself beside him, her arm brushes his as she sits.

Grateful, he takes the leafy dish. "What are the trolls and harvesters like?"

"The trolls are like me, a little. I'm only part troll but they are useful should you have something of value to barter. The harvesters mostly stick to themselves. Unless you die there is no need for them, just hope your soul is pure and goes to Tranquility."

The hairs on her arm stand on end as a chilly breeze carries over them. He wraps an arm over her shoulder. She doesn't complain and leans into him. Electricity softly buzzes through him at her touch. They sit that way as the sun vanishes and the glowing ball of the night comes out. Much less radiant, it offers enough light to see it's joined by a multitude of twinkles covering the sky.

"The moon and stars. You don't have these where you come from, do you?"

"No, all that separates night and day is the temperature. All colors lift from the valley in horizontal rows that only stop when something unthinkable happens." *Like arresting Sulien.*

She sighs. "Tomorrow your new life begins. I will guide you as far as the start of the sand."

He wants to beg her to join them. Her presence is warm and comforting. She is amazing and attractive and her tail brings a smile to her lips every time it sweeps upward in excitement or swings in happiness moving with her laughter, but this is his quest, not hers.

The only thing separating them from the wasteland is a grassy plain surrounded by bright orange flowers Libby calls fox nettle. Libby stands next to Leif and says, "You'll need food for the journey."

REALM WALKER

Leif tilts his head downward and sees something in her hand. A large, folded leaf, by the looks of it bulging at the seams. She lifts it. "These are the most nutritious plants in the treacherous lands and they dry well, making fruit leather."

"Thank you," he says, taking the leaf filled to the brim with green fruit.

"There's caves in the lowlands," she says, pointing toward the falls.

He nods. A moment of silence stands between them, thick in the air.

"You must not walk over the flowers and through the meadow without asking the pixies' permission," Libby warns.

Is it a warning such as the lake of faces in which Sulien survived? A legend that lives through her and others like her, or a real thing? Grass blows gently side to side, nothing menacing about it.

As if she could read his mind, she explains, "The barrier of flowers protects the pixies from creatures in the treacherous lands that might eat them as a fine meal. Devouring a pixie will transfer its magic for a short time. They are a sought-after delicacy for the high they provide even if it's short lived. The flowers turn to scorching winds when breached, consuming the enemy."

Sulien clears his throat and says, "How do we ask?"

Life after Death

It is a logical question and Sulien of all people understands and respects the magical abilities of others, having hidden his necromancy rune all his life.

Libby smiles as if she understands exactly the wheels turning in Sulien's head and responds, "Nothing special. Just ask."

It is Leif's turn. He steps forward to the edge of the orange flowers, sure not to touch even a bushy leaf. "May we pass?"

Nothing happens at first. His eyes reach over the meadow to the desert beyond. After a few slow-moving moments something buzzes in his ear like an insect moving to the back of his head.

Libby, as always, seems to read his mind and places a hand over his as he raises it to swat at whatever insect is buzzing around his head. Her movements suggest *don't* and he *doesn't*. Enjoying her flesh over his he doesn't immediately drop his hand until she gently pushes it downward.

Once his palm is lowered in a non-defensive position the flowers part in front of his feet, similar to how grass and plants move in Aradia. The movement ripples through the grass, opening a trail. Libby nods in confirmation.

He can't leave her quite yet. Taking her hands in his, he thanks her then plants a short kiss on her cheek. She lights up in

Realm Walker

yellow bioluminescence for a moment as if blushing and offers him a smile.

They stay on the path through the meadow until reaching the other side. The sands of the dry, desolate lands shine and twinkle under the reddish sky. Flames ravage his face as the heated air of the land sweeps over them. He glances over his shoulder at Libby before moving forward with Sisimo and Sulien into the place that is their new home.

Life after Death

10

They take Libby's advice and head to the lowlands and Blood Falls. The red sky makes the sun not as horrible as it looks but the wind blows hot and kicks up loose particles of sand into tiny sandstorms that dust their feet and legs. Sisimo flies ahead, searching for a cave or a place to rest for the night.

It's a grueling journey and the satchel is weightier than Leif thought as he trudges through the sand. There is so much sand and, for a moment, his faith in the vision waivers. How can anything live here? Reminding himself of the visionairies' message, he plows on. They have all they need and must follow his instincts.

Sulien pauses, rests the withered branch against his leg, and lowers the cloak he has tied around his mouth to keep the sand out to take a swig of water. Leif stops at his side and coats his throat, careful not to drink too much. The provisions they have won't last long.

Sisimo's wings flap high in the air as he heads towards them. Hope fills Leif that maybe he found a place they can rest for the night. He can't tell what thoughts might be bumping around in Sulien's head but he doesn't watch Sisimo as Leif does. His eyes are on the falls. Sheets of blood pour from the mountain, spilling into the mouth of the river.

"We should move," Leif suggests.

Sulien returns the cloak to cover his mouth from the fine sand blowing steadily in the air and nods.

They don't get far when Sisimo reaches them. Lowering to the ground he nudges Leif's leg. "Did you find something?" he asks, and takes out the water bottle.

The griffon accepts the drink as Leif pours it down his throat. His thirst quenched for the moment he purrs and rises into the air and nods his head. Leif takes that as a yes to his question. The griffon moves forward then pauses as they follow him. His fluffy tail guiding him like a propeller.

The worst thing is by far the wind and heat, but the river isn't fun either. It weaves through the land and is mostly narrow enough for their long legs to jump over. They come to a wider area and pause. Leif pushes against the water with the wind rune, creating a small gap no thicker than his finger. The magic here is weaker and the current of the water stronger than it appears. He tries again with the same result.

"We can walk through it," Sulien says.

The blood soaks through his boots and socks. It's warm and sticky, but the water is shallow, never rising above Leif's knees. Sisimo perches on a rolling, sandy hill and waits as they traipse the river.

They finally reach Sisimo who jumps to the next hill. They follow him. Heading uphill takes more energy and his satchel is getting heavier. At the top of the fourth hill, Sisimo stops and glances down. There's a gap between the hills. It isn't large or a cave but enough they can rest for the night from the grueling wind and sand.

The ground in the gap is hard as stone, but Leif is happy for the protection from the elements. He lowers his satchel and takes out the water bottle, taking another drink, and offers some to the griffon.

Realm Walker

They eat and rest for the night. The red sky turns darker. Its hue always crimson, reflecting the blood of the land.

Two days later…

Wandering the lowlands they find a cave system and make it home, at least for the moment. It's close to Thraves and has three carved compartments. The sand in colored layers of white, yellow, and gold. At the far end, blood trickles through the hardened sand, dropping into a pool surrounded by glassy black and clear stones.

Leif empties the large satchel around Sisimo and his smaller one. They find two large canisters, clothing, and crystals. Sulien uses the items to build a filter system. The blood trickle falls into the top canister layered with sand, the crystals and the clothing sinking into the lower, larger canister.

Leif sets out the remaining alchemy paraphernalia, bowls, medicinal supplies, mortar and pestle, and other sorts of tools for Sulien's trade, and the plants he collected on their journey. The glowing blue flowers no longer glow, but maybe their seeds will be of use. He places them to the side, along with the tiny red heart-shaped flowers with an unknown purpose, and the blooms and seeds he collected from Serenity Tree.

The visionaries said he has all he needs but, looking at the collection, Leif can't think of any way to use the items to bring life from the dead. That is Sulien's job.

Sulien rests his back against the wall and stretches his legs in front of him as he scans the items Leif laid out. He picks up a seed from the tree and holds it between his fingers. It's about the size of a pit and oval shaped. Turning it in various directions, he sets it down. "We'll figure it out, but first we need to figure out how we are going to survive."

"I should make the trip to Verboten. Libby said they will trade."

Sulien gives him a quizzical side-eye. "That journey will take you across the land."

"I think I'll bring these," Leif says, petting the dried red heart flowers. "But what do we need?"

"You should wait a few days, regain your strength, and take the griffon with you," Sulien says, pulling his boots off. His socks are pink from the river.

11

ays turned into more days, and each day Sulien gives Leif an excuse not to make the trip to Verboten, but they won't survive long on the fruit Libby gave them and their provisions from Marsay. Leif hoists his satchel over his shoulder.

"You're leaving," Sulien says. "I can't stop you." His shoulders hunched in defeat, his voice tinged with concern.

"No, it's time."

Sulien lowers his brows and nods. The fatherly side of him wants to protect the young man from a land he isn't sure they should have journeyed to. He's tried to keep his thoughts to himself. He can't bring back any life without life to begin with and the land is dead. "Be careful."

With a nod, Leif exits. Sulien watches Leif and the griffon until they're a dot on the horizon. Turning on his heel, he sees something else. A tall man with a full beard hanging over his chest walking towards him from Thraves. It's a land filled with tall green trees. The sky above is gray with clouds and a golden sheen moves through it from sunlight.

The man waves as if in greeting. A harvester, Sulien assumes, and can't imagine why he is making the dreadful journey into the barren land. Sulien mentioned Leif making the trip to Thraves, but Leif insisted on Verboten based on Libby's suggestion, but seeing this man approaching he thinks maybe it was the wrong choice. Surely with all the green plants the place has water.

Sand kicks up and twirls between them in a funnel before sinking down and blowing across the hill. The man is every bit as tall as Sulien. His thick chestnut hair blows over his shoulder, pushed by the desolate land winds.

"I've come from Thraves. It's not usual to see someone in this land," the man says, a pearl-handled pikestaff in one hand. He rests it in the sand.

It isn't much of a greeting. "Sulien "

"Carlan," the man says, finally introducing himself.

"No, I'm sure it isn't customary. My assistant and I have traveled a distance to get here." A blast of wind kicks up, tossing sand over their heads. "We should go inside."

"I'm here to deliver this," Carlan says, handing him a folded paper with a wax seal stamped with a scythe. "If you are to be our neighbors, our sovereign would like to meet you."

The man's eyes under his bushy brows catch Sulien's attention. The colors swirl in brown, gold, green, and blue. They constantly move around the iris, making Sulien a bit dizzy. "Thank you, can I at least offer you some water?"

They don't have much, Leif took two bottles and there is one left, but it's the neighborly thing to do.

"That's kind, but I should return."

Sulien doesn't argue and is a bit relieved he turns him down.

The unrelenting sands rain against his cloak. Night falls and the red sky gives way to a darker hue. Almost red-black. Leif and

Life after Death

Sisimo put their heads together and curl into each other for warmth and protection. After the day's journey, drinking slowly, they manage one bottle of water and half the dried fruit.

His body quakes in shivers from the cold desert air. His belly screaming for more food, tongue and throat begging for water. His mind drifts to places it shouldn't go. The visionaries told him to trust himself, he had everything he needed to bring life to this place where even insects didn't live and burrow underground.

Is it all a farce to draw him to death? He rethinks the vision, questioning its authenticity. Some warlocks have the ability to read minds and even place thoughts into someone else's mind if they have the runes. Is that what happened, was he tricked?

No! His thoughts shout. Don't think that way. He draws his mind, reels it in, telling himself even warlocks can't place visions into someone else's head unless they are visionaries.

What he saw wasn't a warlock impressing their power of suggestion, but a real vision. Crying out, he screams, "What am I missing?" Sisimo shifts beside him.

Leif understands the visionaries won't respond. They told him once he left Marsay they wouldn't be able to reach him again. He's on his own in a place no one dares go. He thinks of Sulien and wonders how he's faring.

It's those thoughts that warm him, comfort him and draw him into their embrace. Positioning the satchel under his head, Sisimo draws a paw around him, pulling him close, and tucks his beak into the sand, protecting Leif from the bitter cold and bite of the gritty sand blowing on the winds. Sleep comes in moments but it isn't the sleep of a weary traveler.

Life after Death

12

The note contains a hand drawn map showing that Sulien to pass under the falls. The journey doesn't look so far and the harvester who materialized from nowhere didn't seem to have trouble with the terrain.

From the viewpoint on the top of the hill the treacherous lands appears far away, barely visible. Sulien stays on a steady northern course, taking small sips of water only to wet his throat. The golden ground beneath his feet moves as low winds blow it over his shoes.

Realm Walker

The sky more pinkish and the winds dropping off, a gentle splash of running liquid filters into his ears.

The hardened ground is slick with red droplets as the blood river flows away from the mountain. Its mouth wide and gaping and flowing in the life force belonging to the dead. Somewhere in his head he knows the viscous red liquid is the key to bringing life to the realm.

The mountain in the distance doesn't seem far or high. The rocks are less smooth and more jagged the closer to Thraves he gets.

The rocks are slick with blood. He steps carefully, the lull of the falls filling his ears. If he closed his eyes he'd think it was a waterfall in Marsay. His mind evaporating its red hue and metallic odor. A smell he is growing used to.

Rocks stacked on rocks offer a staircase of sorts. Their shiny surfaces show much weathering and are smooth. Some cut in sharp edges.

On steady, wide feet he moves from one smooth rock to the next, avoiding the sharper ones and using the driftwood as a stabilizer.

Each step slow to balance himself. His boots are made to grip and one foot slides as he steps over the jagged tip of a large rock.

It slips and he draws it back. Losing his balance, he teeters for a moment, surveys the path, and takes a wider trail of smoother rocks to his left.

The falls, rich and red, pour from high in the mountains, creating a sheet several meters high. He judges fifty or more.

There isn't a gap or break in the steady sheet of blood raining from the falls into a wide mouth of the narrow river.

A shadow moves on the other side. He sees it through the slivers in the falls. The falls part in the middle. A blood-washed trail of rocks lead to it.

Sulien's eyes meet Carlan's who is holding the pearled pikestaff. The uncongenial man doesn't say anything as Sulien maneuvers over the slick rocks using the driftwood.

Passing through the open curtain, he slips into Thraves. Carlan taps the blood and the falls close, the sheet of blood returning.

Sprinkles of light burst through cracks in the rock, offering enough light to see.

"This way," Carlan says, leading into the mountain. Glowing stalactites and stalagmites rise and fall lighting the way.

Lost in an ocean of golden sand Leif wonders if they'll actually find Verboten and wishes for Libby's guidance.

Realm Walker

She thought their mission a fool's errand and so maybe it is. Sisimo takes wing as Leif urges him into the air to find Verboten.

Conserving energy is essential. Leif sits under his cloak to break the wind and sand.

All they have is enough dried fruit for the day and one bottle of water. That isn't much, and the griffon will need more to rebuild his strength when he returns. He swallows a gulp of water and a slice of the dried fruit from the ones Libby picked for him in the treacherous lands.

The fruit is bitter but filling. He wishes for another swallow to push it down but chooses to save the water for Sisimo.

He continues his southward travels with the cloak pulled around his mouth and somehow, still, tiny shards of sand find their way between his teeth.

The red sky turns gold and he pauses. Hope tickles his insides as his eyes reach through the gold, searching for green, flowers, or any sign of life and Verboten.

It's a mirage. He notices this too late as the golden sky becomes a wall of moving sand. It heads for him and is so wide he can't see around it.

Tucking his satchel close to his chest and pulling his cloak tightly around him and over his face, he faces the wall of sand. Even if magic was stronger here, his rune wouldn't save him.

Sand pelts his cloak like tiny daggers. It fills the space around his feet and legs. Moves to his chest, his neck and finally stops when it covers him completely.

His eyes drawn closed, he pushes against the sand dune that buries him. It's heavy. The sand sinks through his fingers as he pushes it off him, shakes his head. Sand flies around him and a groan rumbles beneath him.

His body suddenly becomes weightless as it drops, the sand too heavy for the ground to bear. Sand slides downward like an hourglass. Darkness swallows him.

He lands on a pillow of sand and opens his eyes. A crevasse about a meter wide, and possibly several meters long, opened and swallowed him.

Red light falls through the crevasse as sand continues to slide downward. Its flow breaking up.

The satchel close to his chest with an iron grip. His first thought is that Sisimo won't find him. Surely he'll see the fresh crack in the dry sand. The thought gives him an idea. He digs through the satchel, pulling out a small metal can filled with the items he brought for trade. Pouring them into his hand, he transfers them to an inside pocket, taking out the couple dried fruit strips.

Realm Walker

He shoots a small blast of plasma into the can and closes the lid. It shines, but for how long? Magic is weak here and he's tired, dehydrated, and hungry. Laying the bottle at an angle so the light will shine onto it. He throws his bag over him and stands. The cavern isn't tall on the sides. It's tall in the middle which is filled with an underground blood brook.

He was heading south and the current in the brook appears to move west. A high pitched squeal, invisible to most ears except animals, leaves his mouth as he uses the sound rune to manipulate the airwaves hoping Sisimo will hear it. Without the strong magic in Marsay he's unsure how far it will reach.

The brook may be his only way out. The sides of the cave low, he has to walk in the middle. Blood soaks through his shoes. He hopes if he follows it long enough it will lead him out.

His eyes burn from the scratchy sand. He dares use a little more magic and pours a small amount of water into his palm, brings it to his eyes and causes a gentle breeze to spray. It helps, but doesn't completely take the sand away. He used enough magic already and doesn't dare use any more. When he makes it to Verboten he will rinse well with the fresh water in the realm. He has no way to give Sisimo a message.

Life after Death

Gathering as much spit as his mouth musters, barely enough to swallow, it goes down like razor blades from the sand in his mouth.

13

A long table is spread with meat, fruit, vegetables, and breads. Sulien's stomach gurgles at the delicacies and he accepts some of everything, not willing to let a hearty meal go, yet not greedy.

Six others, all harvesters, sit around the table. The sovereign at the head. He is as tall as any harvester with hair as long as any and a beard to match the others. His clothing is a simple gray tunic and matching pants. There is nothing special about his appearance, except he is as neat and clean as the others and Sulien is a mess. Sand coats his salt and pepper hair, the unshaven mask of hair on his face, and sticks to his clothing. There isn't enough water to bathe or clean their clothing.

They manage three bottles of water a day through the filter. It's barely enough for them to exist. The griffon has flown to these lands and returned with edible plants that help but, overall, it is quite an unbearable existence.

"What is it you want with such a vile land? It's dead, nothing can grow or live there," the sovereign asks, his tone demanding but curious.

Sulien wants to drink the entire tall glass of water but chooses to sip instead. He weighs the sovereign's words but has nothing to lose. "I want to fill the land with a life that can subsist on the one resource it has."

"Blood?" a harvester, introduced as Sampa, asks with a light chuckle. He is older, his brown hair peppered with gray and white.

"Yes."

"They would have to really want blood. It is a harsh land," the sovereign says. His words aren't light. He means them.

The life would need indeed to love, even crave, blood. His eyes meeting the sovereign's. The colors of his irises chasing each other. All harvesters are made that way it seems. "Tell me about what you do." Sulien says, not to change the subject but to work a deal. Maybe they can help each other.

Realm Walker

"We harvest the souls of the dead, sending them to their afterlife," a female says, her hair as thick and brown as the men's but her face smooth and taut. She's young and the sovereign's daughter.

"Where do these souls come from?"

"The outer realm," she responds, her gaze flicking to her father who gives her a slow, approving nod. She isn't beautiful but isn't unattractive, more a handsome type of young woman.

The place some warlocks ventured to many centuries past. They were explorers of the realms, some stayed in the middle realms and others went further. He and the harvesters are descendants of these people known in Marsay as realm walkers. That makes them kin. "And what of their bodies?"

"We don't know," the older harvester says. "Our job is their souls, not their physical form."

The sovereign swirls the liquid in his glass, eyes watching the movement. "You want to create life from the dead." His gaze lifts, meeting Sulien's. The intensity almost makes him look away.

"I do," he says and a whisper tickles his ear. *Tell him what you are.* Other than Leif he's never told another, but this is a different land and these people work with the dead. They are caretakers of them, same as Sulien. The words come out with more strength than he thought possible. "I am a necromancer. I raise the dead."

A rush of power rises over his spine and prickles his neck. He has never used the ability to raise a person and with the lack of magic in the area he knows it will take more than a large sacrifice, but a tool to amplify the magic. His mind spins and he feels the rune heat with his thoughts.

The harvesters don't bat an eye at his words. They don't shun him or curse him. Not a single one has risen to tie him to a pyre.

A harvester who's been quiet through most of the meal speaks, a spot of bread on his beard: "You think we can work together. We supply you bodies and you fill them with magic?"

Not exactly, but something like that, only he needs the dead with souls. A dead person without a soul has no empathy. Clarity like that of a fine diamond smacks him, and he understands. The army of the dead the last Marsayan necromancer made failed. They had no souls, were nothing more than moving corpses. "Their souls need to be intact or they will have no empathy, no concern for life, or desire for the blood that flows through the realm. Nothing more than empty shells."

The sovereign leans back in his chair, not from the hearty meal but in contemplation. His hands folded over his abdomen. "I'm not sure we can make a bargain. Souls belong to one of two afterlives: Tranquility or the Otherworld. There are consequences if those souls don't pass on."

Life after Death

14

The cave grows dark, light from the crevasse no longer visible. Leif's eyes are partially adjusted to the darkness. His other senses work harder. The cave is cooler than above ground, with many small caverns. He trudges on thinking there isn't an end. The brook he's following as windy as the river above. He calls the griffon again, nearly bumping his forehead on the ceiling. Seeing the dense shadow at the last second, he ducks.

Realm Walker

The passageway growing narrower and shorter. No longer able to stand, he lowers to his hands and knees, not too proud to crawl through sand muddied with blood. It gathers between his fingers and crawls under his nailbeds and the metallic scent wrinkles his nose. It's much stronger in the cave. The narrowing and darkening cave becomes lower until he's on his belly, slithering and blind, and thinks maybe he should turn around. Surely this isn't a way out for him.

His brain barely registers the thought when his body slides downhill, headfirst. A pin of white brightens as he drops. Light, he thinks when his shoulder hits something hard. The slick blood pushes him past it and the pin prick turns blue, pink, and purple. Focused on the changing colors, he doesn't see the large stone until his head smashes into it. All the colors leave his vision as he passes out. His mind returning to darkness.

Carlan doesn't escort Sulien out of Thraves, but deeper into it. The walls inside the mountain are smooth and carved. Steps and rooms fashioned from stone. He follows Carlan through a corridor and into the evening light. It's dark with stars and a moon, reminding him of the treacherous lands and Aradia. During the day, Thraves wears a sky of gray clouds but during the night it's bright and flashy.

The grass and trees are green. There are no shiny flowers of any color or shimmering bugs buzzing in the air. Carlan pushes a door open and they enter another cave. There are two chairs with a table between them. Light from a candle flickers in a glass-like cage unlike the lights of Marsay. They use plasma. It is magic bestowed on every warlock. The first rune they receive; a simple lightning bolt.

"Marcus will be with you," Carlan says and exits the way he came. It seems Carlan is of lower status, merely a messenger for the higher ranking.

Light dances from another room until darkness moves in front of it. A man stands in the doorway, looking much like every other harvester. Even his clothing is dull. The man's beard lifts as his lips curl. "I'm Marcus," he says, striding into the room and taking the other seat.

"Sulien."

"Yes, a necromancer." He folds his hands, much like the sovereign did, over his abdomen. "You want to raise the dead and make a home for them in the desolate land."

How does he know this? He didn't attend the lunch and not much time has passed. Only enough to get from the room to this one. The meal did take a few hours. He lifts his brows. "I think it can work."

The man's mustache lifts as his lips meet a full smile. "I think you're right. You see, I'm the head harvester. I know everyone on the list to be harvested. The people of the outer realm are violent."

Those words make Sulien cringe. Some of those people are warlocks, or were. No doubt not a true warlock anymore, especially if their blood is mingled with common outerrealmers – humans.

"They murder each other ruthlessly with axes and swords, chopping off heads and body parts. They are lost in a land with no magic. It's a land of lost souls, of a people riddled with a need to kill and we have a hard time keeping up. The sovereign doesn't like to hear it, but it's quite true. We don't have the manpower for all the souls we send on, and some get lost. We can't harvest them in time and their spirits roam the realm with no purpose. I think you can help us."

Sulien came to Thraves out of options. The invitation to the realm and this deal give the reason he and Leif left Marsay real. It swells and fizzes inside him as they work out the deal. He will be allotted five humans a week once he learns to travel into the outer realm and learns their ways. The realm Marcus calls the land of lost souls.

Life after Death

Sulien accepts the deal, knowing he doesn't know how he's going to give the humans life after death, especially if he has to do so in a land without magic. The small animal in Aradia took a drop of blood. What will a human take?

If he can get them to the desolate land, then he can use the blood of the river. His thoughts are interrupted as Marcus says, "I will give you one of the most skilled harvesters to work with. He is young and doesn't play by the rules. Until I figure out what else to do with him, he's yours." His lips curl into a sly smile. "I think the two of you will work nicely together."

15

A searing pain shoots through Leif's collarbone and his head throbs. He lifts an arm to his collarbone, as if touching it will make the pain go away. It is a familiar pain. He opens his eyes. Colorful light spills through a curtain that blows inward from a gentle breeze. The walls of the room are wood. There's a table to his right and a blanket pulled to his chin.

The new surroundings don't erase the dream. It was more than a dream. The jarring pain that knocked him out also brought a vision of a tool. Its jade handle smooth and

Life after Death

cold in his hand. Its head is a sharp curve with jagged edges made from an iron-like metal. *Life takes great sacrifice.* The four words echo in his head. Three faceless dead lay in a sea of shimmering sand. Their chests still, bodies like boards. He stands over them with the tool. The jade handle in his hand. Heat swelters in the air around the teeth, shimmering under the red sky. Blood rain pelts against their bodies and, one by one, they rise.

There was something unnatural about their movements as they sped away from him with incredible speed. The pain simmers in his collarbone. The familiar pain like an old friend. He glances downward, lifting the blanket, and sees the tool in his vision stare back at him in black.

A new rune, not Sulien's. *The scythe of immortality* whispers through the air. He gulps with the realization. It is he who will breathe life into bodies able to live in the harsh, unforgiving land. The serenity and satisfaction he expected to feel when he too became a necromancer, the thing he'd longed for, isn't what he felt. A part of him is sickened, his stomach nauseous and hands clammy.

"Look who decided to wake up," a familiar voice announces from the doorway as a short female enters the room. Her long, dark hair draped over her shoulder in a braid and her cute lavender and pink feathery tails swaying in emotion. She carries something in her hand.

His body vibrates in the excitement of seeing Libby. A face he didn't think he'd ever lay eyes on again. Only a step or two behind her, Sisimo pushes through the open doorway. Immediately stalking towards the bed, he lays his head on the mattress, his beak resting against Leif's leg and fluffy tail swinging under his back legs.

"You're lucky, you know. He carried you to the village and deposited you at my feet."

So much, so soon, his mind bubbles in excitement while something dark remains shadowed in the corner. Lifting a hand he touches the head of the animal. "I knew you'd hear me, follow my clue and my voice."

She leans over him and lays whatever she's carrying on his head. "Welcome to Verboten, land of the rainbow sky. You hit that noggin of yours on a diamond as big as your foot. You have quite a lump and shouldn't get up. The poultice should have the swelling down by tomorrow. If you're hungry I can bring you food."

Hungry. Yes! His head throbs like the marching band of village people thronging Sulien, and his collarbone burns like griffon fire, but his stomach screams for something to fill it.

Life after Death

She returns with soup, bread, and water on a tray. He pushes himself up. The poultice drops. The lump on his head arguing with the pain as daggers stab his skull. Each time he opens his mouth for a bite the daggers dig in and sharp pains radiate through his head. Sopping the bread in the soup, he doesn't have to open his mouth wide to eat, and is thankful she brought soup and bread instead of meat.

Libby scoots a chair he hadn't noticed from a spot against the wall to the side of the bed. "Have you given up?" she asks with too much glee.

"No, not at all. I came to trade." The items in the pocket of his bag will do nicely, he hopes, to get the metal and jade he needs to fashion the scythe.

She props her tiny feet onto the bed and Sisimo curls around her chair like a traitor. "What did you bring and what do you need? Maybe I can help you."

He doesn't doubt she can. "The red flowers from the treacherous lands and sap imbued with magic. I was hoping to trade it for items to build a filter and a large canister to hold the filtered blood, but I also need a metal like iron and jade and someone who can smith."

"You're not looking for much," she scoffs. "I think I can help." The lilt in her words betray her thoughts as there is no surprise or questioning tone in her voice. He asks himself, not for the first time, if she can read his thoughts. "Those red heart flowers are worth a lot and the sap might go over well. What kind of magic?"

"Youthfulness of spirit and wrinkle reducer." He chose those as they were always a big hit in Marsay.

"Trolls can be vain. I'll see what I can do. You rest." She pulls her feet off the bed and drops to the floor. Stretching over him, she grabs the poultice and lays it on the table. "Put this on when you lay down. The Aradian herbs will make you good as new." Her two-toned tail feathers bounce with her steps. Sisimo follows at her heel.

"Traitor," Leif says as he gently lowers his head to the pillow and props the poultice over the massive lump.

16

Kymani isn't as large as the average harvester but is every bit as tall as Sulien, and the colors in his eyes are stable. They don't swirl, but his pupils are slits and his irises golden like a wild animal's. His long, dark, thick hair shaved above his ears with one long braid in the middle. It is as full and thick as any harvester's. "I use stones. A stone from each realm I belong to works to trap loose souls. The ones that get away from the harvesters," he says, his voice distant yet profound. He empties a small bag of stones into his palm. "I use these to harvest and portal."

"Portal?" Sulien asks.

Kymani's lip rises on the left in a crooked smile. "To Lols. It's a better mode of travel, much quicker."

Sulien's mind sorts the words. Portalling is a way of travel. Not one he quite understands, but assumes he will soon. Lols, on the other hand, is a place and it strikes him. Marcus's words: he called it a land of lost souls. The ah hah moment sweeps over his face.

"First you need the basics on what I do," Kymani says and lifts the scythe he's been resting his weight on. "Once I trap the soul, I use this." He lifts the scythe, its handle made of a polished, shiny metal and the head made from a type of red rock. "Ansa."

"You portal and go to them," Sulien says, more for clarification. "Can the portal bring them here?"

Kymani's strange eyes widen, the black slits narrow. "No, we don't want them here. We harvest their souls to keep them out of the middle realms. Most harvesters don't go there in their physical form. They harvest in their spirit form, but I can't. I'm a hybrid." His statement reflects pride, as he's something slightly different. It reflects the tone he used on the word 'harvester' earlier, like he doesn't

quite belong and thinks of himself as
something more.

He skirts the question and Sulien takes
the answer as a yes. "The desolate land is
brutal. They wouldn't survive on their own."

A long sigh leaves Kymani's lips. "I
wouldn't be so sure. They are violent and
appear to enjoy torture."

That makes Sulien's job more difficult,
but if he can learn how to portal he can bring
them back on his own. First, he needs to
figure out how to bring back the dead, fresh
dead.

The stones laid in a specific order,
Kymani stands in the center. "We're doing
this." He waves a hand for Sulien to join him.
The stone circle is large enough for the two of
them and Ansa.

Ansa isn't small as she rests in a
scabbard on Kymani's back. The head
reaching above his. The small bag he carries
the stones in tied to his belt. People have to
notice her, even violent ones. Brutal people
might concern themselves with someone
carrying such a large weapon.

As if Kymani reads his mind, he says,
"They all carry weapons. You'll see."

Kymani lays one rock down with the
others and a light flashes around them. It's
teal and warm. When it dissolves they're no
longer in Thraves or the desolate land but the
outer realm. The land of lost souls. The dense

woods filled with green bushy trees and wildflowers. Kymani walks like he knows where he's going. "Tell me about where you're from."

"It's mountainous. They reach into the sky and are covered with a steady fog. Waterfalls drop into more waterfalls and pools of water. Caves and tunnels fill the inside of the mountains, with embedded crystals in the walls. Color rises from the valley and fills the sky with colors. The atmosphere is thick and heady with magic," Sulien says. He realizes how much he misses the land and its beauty, but not the people.

"What are those?" Kymani asks, pointing to Sulien's arm. Earlier, he rolled his sleeves up and he must have seen.

"Runes. They are marks concentrated with magic. Each rune associates with a different skill."

"Like necromancy," the words roll from Kymani's tongue as if it's nothing. Not a skill that nearly burned him on a pyre, but another magic like all others. He's wanted this moment and it feels good.

Sulien stops and kneels down. Using a rock, he traces the symbol of his necromancer mark: a circle chasing another to no end. Two circles never-ending, symbolizing that the cycle of life and death has no beginning or end. "Like that."

Life after Death

Kymani studies it for a moment. "Infinity."

Yes, the cycle repeats forever.

The trees become more sparse. "Stay here and watch." Kymani empties the stones into his hand and walks several feet east and stops. He lays the stones on the ground in a different configuration than the one used to open a portal. He doesn't step inside as he lifts Ansa from the scabbard. The red rock lights up and for a moment a black blob is visible as it comes in contact with her. Once the blob is loose of the scythe it vanishes and Kymani collects the rocks and returns to Sulien.

"I have another couple to fetch, not far, but won't be as easy to stomach."

Sulien's glad he saved that one for last as he follows Kymani through the woods until they come upon a bloody field. The grass looks like the blood river in the desolate land and Sulien is more sure these people are the ones he needs. They must enjoy blood enough to live in a land with nothing else. There are no bodies or weapons. He watches on as Kymani does his harvesting trick again. The circle of stones larger and three zaps to the red rock head and he's done.

They follow a trail out of the woods. "Ever see a blood bath like that?" Kymani asks.

Realm Walker

"No. These are the people I need. Ones who crave blood."

"That they do."

The sun lowers in the sky with a vibrant display. Its earlier blue changing to slashes of several colors. The trail ends in a small village. Its homes not so different than Marsay. Kymani pushes the doors open to a place filled with voices. Sulien almost gasps when he sees the people. Men mostly with long hair and beards. They're dirty, filthy, like Sulien, and stink. He finds it strange people choose filth. He knows there is water, as they passed a stream in the woods. As Kymani said, most have visible weapons. Knives sheathed at their sides. Swords on their backs. None have a scythe, but weapons they do. They are a strange and violent people. He remembers the sovereign's words and Kymani mirroring the words of warning.

They find a table. Kymani leans an elbow on it and it rocks. His pupils enlarged, allowing in more light inside the darkened pub. "The drink is grainy and well…I think I'd rather drink blood, but you have to drink it to fit in."

His words don't give Sulien any confidence in their taste buds, but they assure him the desolate land might be just the place for such people.

The patrons in the establishment seem happy, if not as disgusting in appearance as

Life after Death

Sulien. If anyone stands out its Kymani, with his freshly bathed skin and clean clothing. His neatly braided hair and stubble-free face. A woman with several layers to her gown joins them. She stands near the table, two wooden drinks in her hands, liquid sloshes over the side. She drops them on the table.

"You're back," she says, "tell me about your travels." Her tone syrupy with bite. They have a relationship. One she both enjoys and dislikes.

Kymani's lip lifts as he leans back and takes her in. She's attractive, with long blonde hair tied in a bun, curls everywhere. Her blue eyes glitter. "What time?" Kymani asks.

"I've been waiting for you honey," she says, in a not-so-private eye conversation as her cerulean orbs move from his face to his lap and plant themselves. Kymani's seem to rest on her burgeoning chest and visible cleavage.

Kymani offers her a wink and turns toward Sulien. "You got this, right?" He lifts Ansa from his back. "Keep an eye on her and don't kill anyone."

From the shifty smile on his face, Sulien can already tell he is up to something. Most likely her thighs and breasts.

Sulien rests the scythe against his leg. He's glad Kymani is gone for the moment. Next to him, even though similar heights, he feels small and awkward. Ansa weighs more than he thought and thinks the handle is made from iron – the metal of life – and the red stone, he thinks, has meaning too. Perhaps it is cinnabar. It gives him an idea.

To raise the dead in a land with little or no magic he needs something to amplify it and has just the thing at home in the cave. The driftwood symbolizes the bridge between life and death, but that's only part of what he needs. Carlan had a pearl walking stick he used to part Blood Falls. Thraves has pearls and pearls represent the cycle of life.

17

Leif wakes up. A slim band of light filtering into the room from the open window. His head doesn't throb as much. His eyes fix to the ceiling and watch the colors dance across it. His mind urging him to sleep more, but his eyes have other ideas. It isn't day, but it isn't night. Either the wee hours of the morning or the settling evening.

In the desolate land the sky is always red. Varying shades of red, but always red. In the early morning it's a deep crimson, lightening with every minute until it's a reddish pink. By the evening, it turns crimson again. He notes he's alone as he rises from his bed. Not even Sisimo joins him. He decides it must be evening or Sisimo would be there curled on the floor near him.

There isn't much furniture in the room. There's the bed, the chair Libby sat on, and the small table beside the bed. Pants are folded across the wooden back of the chair. He sits up, sliding his legs over the mattress to the floor. When he stands, a wave of dizziness rushes through him and he drops onto the edge of the bed until it passes.

After several minutes, he tries again. This time dizziness doesn't come, but he nearly hits his head again on the low ceiling made for small people. He slides the pants on – they rise above his ankles – and picks up the shirt underneath them and pulls it over his head. When he does, he feels the knot on his head. It isn't as large as Libby made it out to be, or maybe the poultice did the trick. A pair of shoes with fresh socks laid on top are under the chair. He slides them out and slips them on his feet. They fit. Better than the too-short pants and tight shirt.

When he opens the door, he nearly hits his head again, remembering at the last minute to duck as he moves into the hallway. It's slender, and voices filter through the air. He follows the voices and finds Libby sitting at a table, a drink in her hands, a plate of food in front of her, and an older woman across the table. Sisimo lays curled on the floor. His head lifts when Leif enters the kitchen.

Griffons aren't the largest animals, but they're good sized, and Sisimo, even curled, takes up a decent portion of the room.

Libby and the older woman's gazes drift to Leif.

"Sit down, dear boy, and I'll fix you a plate," the older woman says, her tail feathers sweeping the air behind her.

"Thank you," he says, taking the seat next to Libby.

"I'm glad you're up. We have things to do today." She stands and riffles through his hair, her fingers gliding over the lump. "Much better." Shivers move through him with her touch as they sift through his hair.

Over a breakfast of meat rolled into finger-like structures and fruit, Libby introduces him to the woman she calls her gran-mo.

"I found a buyer for the sap. He'll trade iron for it," Libby says, bouncing on her feet along the dirt path.

The village is made of tiny homes and filled with tiny people all with expressive tail feathers of all colors. They ruffle and fluff and move like feathery appendages. Libby's bounce with her steps, in sync with her feet. Her plumage is shorter. The lavender and pink colors dispersed randomly throughout.

Realm Walker

"Is everyone short?" he asks. Libby is nearly a head taller than the tallest troll he'd seen.

"Don't let it fool you. Trolls don't have height, but they are strong."

Boulders of precious gems and metals poke from the grass, some large enough for him to sit on. Vertical lights flow through the atmosphere, sending a wave of longing coursing through Leif, reminding him of Marsay with its rainbow of colors spreading horizontally in the air from the source. The trees are green and the grass tall enough it sways with the breeze.

Sisimo follows behind. As an animal of the air and land, he isn't grounded. In the time they've spent in the desert, he's flown into Thraves for juicy morsels of a leaf he prefers. For a moment Leif wished he could fly and see all that Sisimo does.

"We didn't bring anything to carry the iron," he says, the thought suddenly forming in his head.

Libby doesn't pause or miss a step. "We don't need it," she says with confidence.

A few cottages outside the village, they turn, staying on a dirt path leading to a wooden structure that looks more like a stable for animals than a place to bargain for metals.

When they reach the door, she raps a couple times and the door opens. Inside, the place is filled with various metals. A young troll greets them. His blue tail feathers stand in alert when his eyes move up Leif and plant themselves on his face.

Libby prances inside while Leif remembers to duck. The ceiling is high inside but the doorway is made for short people.

"Where's Mortan?" Libby asks.

"He had errands. Do you have the sap?" the troll asks. His words pointed and tail feathers wiggling to his side.

"Umm hmm. But we need to see the iron."

The troll's eyes narrow on her as if he doesn't trust her and Leif watches her. The wheels in her mind spin as she seems to size up the troll. He wonders, not for the first time, if she reads minds. "You show me the sap and I'll show you the iron."

She nudges a gentle elbow at Leif's gut. He doesn't need words to understand that means he needs to collect the sap from the satchel around Sisimo, who is too large to fit through the door.

"At the same time," she says, her words and tail reflecting she doesn't fully trust him.

Sisimo sits on his haunches as Leif opens the flap and pulls out two bottles of sap, one for youth and another for wrinkles, and a small bag. He opens it and spots the red heart-shaped flowers from the treacherous lands. Iolida, Libby called them. Returning the bag, he juggles the bottles and drops the flap. When he returns, the troll stands near a counter, a metal cart behind him and its handle clutched tightly in his grip.

Leif lays the bottles on the counter and the troll rolls the cart to him then says, "The cart rental will cost more."

Libby's face contorts. "No, it won't. That's Mortan's deal. We borrow it for the day and return it tomorrow."

The troll waves it off. "That's not my deal."

"This isn't your deal. We bring it back tomorrow," she says with finality, her tone saying more than the words. She made the deal with a different troll and won't be double-crossed.

The troll's eyes flick to Leif, then he pushes the cart towards him. Leif takes it before the troll changes his mind.

"What was that about?" Leif asks once they return to the trail.

"Mortan's son. He's always like that, trying to renege on his father's deals, but he knows his father won't stand for it. Trolls like the bargain, but once the deal is made they are true to their word."

"You handled him well," Leif offers, not knowing what else to say. This is her world, not his. He is small and insignificant here.

Life after Death

"You know, you can probably get anything you want here for the Iolida. The trolls love precious metals, gems, and the rarest of the rare, but won't travel to the land between the realms. They fear it."

But she doesn't? Is that her value in Verboten? A child of two realms, she passes through the treacherous lands carefully, gingerly making it through each obstacle with practiced ease.

True to her words, the sight of a single red heart-shaped Iolida brings a large smile to the round face of a troll she calls Mercari. "For two, I'll throw in Shungite. It makes an excellent filter as it has the right amount of porosity and catches contaminates."

Leif eyes the black stones he calls Shungite and the wealth of metal devices in the room. It seems he can make many things. "Would you fashion a tool made of specific materials for four?"

"Deal," Mercari says without even asking the materials. The small red flowers have much value in Verboten and he wonders what he'll do with flowers from Serenity Tree. No, those aren't for selling but spelling. The vision hadn't shown him, but his head and heart think to give the tool any use it needs the flowers, or at least he shouldn't use them until he knows for sure. The reason he unconsciously kept them. *You have everything you need and intent*, whispers through his soul.

18

redging through the fjord in Thraves, staying in the shallower area, Sulien collects the loose pearls. Kymani was right. He rakes his hand along the bottom of the basin, dirt collecting in his hands alongside pearls. They are embedded in the loose soil and the deeper he goes the more he finds.

The water feels nice against his skin. It's cool and refreshing. Setting the bag full of pearls on the shore, he takes a swim further out and dunks his head, hoping to remove all the caked-on sand. The shivers and bite of the chilly water continue when he steps onto the shore, his clothes soaked head to toe. Grabbing the canister he brought, he dips it in the water and fills it.

The mouth of the fjord is a day's walk from the desolate land. Most of the walk is through Thraves, where the temperatures are cool and the sky overcast. He takes the path under Blood Falls, through the mountain which empties at the mouth of the fjord. Before his return journey, he rests inside the cave. Glowing stalactites drop from the cave ceiling and matching stalagmites jut from the floors. They light the way as he returns.

He doesn't have time to spare as he fashions the pearls into a handle and smooths the driftwood into a head for his scythe. Holding the finished piece, he marvels at his handywork and finishes it with a spell. He dips the wooden head into the river, using the blood as a sacrifice, and says, "Death isn't the end. It is the beginning. Souls will attach and return to whence they came."

Music and dance fill the village as the trolls celebrate the change of seasons. Their tail plumage swinging and springing as they sway to the music. Large gems at the town

Life after Death

square serve as seats, and sweet drinks and various foods are spread over tables. Libby is as rambunctious as any troll as she grabs Leif's hand and shows him the dance. They swing and twirl through the night. Darkness surrounds them and the ever-present colors of the atmosphere are visible through the lights in the square.

Exhausted, he takes a seat on a bright green gemstone to catch his breath. It is the only one not taken. Libby takes the liberty of falling onto his lap, an arm around his shoulder. Her scent is sugary as sap. The touch of her arm over his neck and hand pressed against his shoulder elicit tingles of excitement over his skin that bloom in his soul.

A chunk of dark hair falls over her cheek. He brushes it back and relishes the softness of her skin. Her eyes meet his, twinkling sky, moonlight framing her face. Her lips part slightly. He clasps the tips of her fingers in his hands. Her heartbeat thumps in his ears, increasing in excitement and the bioluminescent glow radiates subtly from her skin. In the months he's spent in the middle realms the magic around them wasn't so complete as it is right now.

She wants what he does. When he presses his lips to hers she meets them, applying her own pressure as they lose themselves in the kiss. Swells of emotion sprout inside him and grow at an alarming rate. When they release, she brushes a hand over his lips and smiles. Her tail feathers brush over his arm and her glow warms him, excites him. He doesn't say anything, as he knows she'll blush and her light will stop shining.

The music and energy of the celebration are over. Most trolls have returned home. It's only them and a handful of other trolls. She hops off his lap, holding a hand for him to clasp, and together they return to her gran-mo's.

The house is quiet. Their lips meet again with less abandon. Their hands clasped as she leads him through the tiny kitchen, narrow hall, and into her bedroom. He runs his hands from her neck and over her arms, then slips them behind her back as he leans his head downward and fills himself with her kiss. She tugs his shirt upwards, He catches it and her hands roam the tight muscles of his chest and abdomen and wander to his belt which they unbuckle.

He finishes what she started and stands in front of her naked while he pushes her shirt over her head, dropping kisses on her bare chest. Her breasts are small, with perfect dime Serenity seed-sized, round nipples. He lifts her light, tiny body up, her legs wrapping around his waist as they fall backwards onto her bed. Her skin glows and

Life after Death

Leif says nothing. It attracts and excites him, even though she is bashful of it. Flesh to flesh, they explore and kiss, finding pleasure in each other.

REALM WALKER

19

Julien swallows hard as he stares at the bodies strewn on the blood-bathed ground. The battle fresh enough the bodies haven't been cleared. He remembers the young girl, Seran, his heart sinking like a brick. He wanted to help her. He could have saved her. These bodies on the field are beyond help. The last of their souls harvested as Kymani gathers them and sends them to their afterlife.

Life after Death

A dark soul is unclean and goes to the Otherworld. The bright souls are pure and go to Tranquility. The souls that zap Ansa are dark and murky. The stench of the decayed bodies isn't one he thinks will ever leave his clothing or nose. It buries itself into his subconscious, attaching to his own soul. The body near his feet a young man, barely more than a child. The sword in his hands covered in blood.

A female voice whispers in his brain: *Take the sword and the knife. Things of this world will return you to it.* It's too late for this young man. He is gone, his body harvested. He won't mind if Sulien takes the sword. Its blade is sharp, and buried in the hilt is an oval amber stone the size of a large seed. In alchemy, amber represents air. It balances.

The young man's dead hands tight around the sword, it takes effort for Sulien to pull it from his grasp. He also takes the knife plunged into the dead boy's back. It is no wonder so much blood drains into Blood Falls, as he's come to call it, in recent days. Hundreds of dead lie at his feet, strewn through a gully. The mountainous midlands rising high above them.

Lols seems to be a land of many faces. This one is dry as the desolate lands and the sun grueling, unlike the crimson sky he's grown used to. It doesn't stave off the heat, but it shadows the sun.

Realm Walker

"I'm done here," Kymani says as he hoists Ansa into the scabbard.

They walk through an opening between the mountains, their heads shielded from the sun, and come out to a home. It sits alone and seems such a lonely place. Lonely as the desolate land except for the trees. With no apparent water source, Sulien wonders how they grow. Is the water beneath the surface? The trees aren't many but, as they near the home, he notes fruit hanging from them. The person who lives here will die within the next couple hours and it will be his turn to use the scythe he fashioned.

Beyond the home, in the far distance, is a great wall surrounding a city. He assumes the bloody battle was between them and another group not far away.

A man collects the fruit, placing them in a basket, a scarf over his head. He welcomes them and offers water. The man with his thick beard is vibrant. The muscles in his chest show he is fit. It seems unlikely he will die soon.

It isn't him, Sulien soon learns, as the man invites them inside. This small gesture shows him not all souls in Lols are violent and black, some are kind and generous. The small home is made of brick and mud and stone. A woman lays on a cot, her dark hair falling over the edges.

Life after Death

"That is my wife," the man says, inviting them to sit at his table and eat bread and fruit.

"It's kind of you," Kymani says, relaxing in the chair.

The inside of the home is cool compared to the heat outside. The brick and mud work similar to the cave he and Leif chose as home.

Kymani offers to help the man collect the fruit, leaving Sulien alone with the woman. He mouths *soon* to Sulien before walking outside into the heat. He rests Ansa against the inside wall near the door. The woman mumbles in her sleep, sweat glistening on her cheeks and forehead. If he had his saps he could probably save her, but in this harsh land without magic all he has is the scythe he fashioned.

She coughs a few times, her chest heaves and falls. Fever consumes her as she breathes her last. His instincts want to save her, call the husband, but that's not why he's here. He can't keep her alive any more than the husband can, but maybe he can return her life. Holding the scythe over her, he touches it against her chest. When nothing happens, he glances at Ansa and picks her up. She is weighty in his hands, a glowing white ball attaches itself to her, taking him by surprise. He holds the scythe, eyes wide as he determines what to do with her soul. He isn't

118

a harvester and the white ball appears content on the scythe as it sticks like glue.

He leans down, Ansa in one hand and collects the scythe he fashioned. He touches the head against the white ball then lowers it toward her body, and something he never expected happens. It takes the shape of the body it belongs to, but in translucent form, hovering over her physical being. Her mouth opens and words fall: "Tell him I love him."

The ethereal form of the woman rises into the air and vanishes through the roof. He wants to run outside and see if she's really gone, then remembers she's dead. The husband will be heartbroken. He returns Ansa to where Kymani left her and runs outside. "Come quick," he calls to the man.

Sulien mourns with the man as he leans over his wife. Kymani urges him out the door so the man may mourn in peace. It all happened so fast, as Sulien sorts why his scythe didn't work. Shock. He didn't expect to see a spirit but a glowing sphere.

They try again and again. The next time he asks Kymani to harvest the soul, since he is a harvester, and considers that trying to complete it all himself without proper harvesting credentials is the problem, but when the same thing happens he rethinks it once more.

The blood he used was from the river, but maybe since the sacrifice wasn't given for life but in the name of a bloody battle, it didn't work. Kymani suggests an animal, and with the sword Sulien salvaged from the dead, he throws it like a javelin catching the animal in the stomach. It falls and crushes Sulien's heart. He couldn't have done that, and now he must give the suffering animal the death blow.

Pulling the sword, the animal's dark eyes blink. He feels its pain and Kymani lifts it onto the stump of a dead tree over Sulien's scythe and makes the death blow saying, "Thank you for your sacrifice so another can live." Tears drop from his eyes as the animal sinks into its final sleep.

Its blood soaks into the driftwood through its crevices.

He tries again. Kymani pulls the soul from the body and Sulien presses the sacrifice-soaked head of his scythe against it and, like the other times, an ethereal form appears. Sulien wields the scythe to catch it but, like the others, it drifts away. His scythe doesn't return a soul to its physical form but pulls it into a spirit form resembling the physical. It reverses the harvesting process and the soul continues its final journey.

20

eif crosses Sulien's mind as he melts the metal in the sword and pours it over the mold he made. It's been weeks since he left and Sulien is beginning to wonder if he survived the harsh land. He jots down his notes as the metal cools, then holds the two halves of the gear-like ascendant in his hands. If it works with the amber stone he found it will portal him to Lols.

The next day, he makes the journey to Thraves to update Marcus on his progress at Marcus's own request. The sky in Thraves only bright over Blood Falls where the perpetual clouds end. Sulien lets out a sigh as Carlan isn't sent to part the falls, so he determines he may be able to slide under from the right and catch the least amount of blood, not that it matters. His clothing is permanently soiled with sand, as well as his hair. The fine particles attach themselves to everything and are found everywhere in the desolate land.

Marcus opens the door to his office and doesn't ask Sulien to sit instead of stand, so the blood droplets on his pants don't stain the chair. He offers him a glass of water. He doesn't refuse. Even the filtered water has a tinge of metallic taste, or maybe that's his senses, always smelling blood.

The day Sulien met Marcus he introduced himself as the lead harvester. The man in charge, who knows the moment souls are harvested. That day, Sulien didn't think to pay attention to the surroundings of the room. Today, he observes the room with a different eye.

An eye of need. If he is to go to Lols alone then he needs to know when the next will die. He scans the room and notes a table along the wall. A candle in a globe sits on top, but there is a drawer beneath. It is the only other furniture besides the chairs and the table between them.

Realm Walker

"Kymani tells me your success is minimal," Marcus says in a tone that reflects he isn't surprised.

Sulien doesn't assume Kymani hasn't told him the truth. In fact, he feels maybe they didn't want him to be successful. "No, the tool I created doesn't return the soul to the body. I've been working on another design." He doesn't tell him the design is a device to portal him to Lols alone, or what he plans on doing when he gets there.

Marcus smooths his hands over his pants leg and crosses one leg over the other. "The tool pulls the soul from the sphere?"

"Yes."

"And the spirit continues on to the afterlife?"

Saying it the way he does makes the scythe seem ridiculous, makes him feel foolish that he, a necromancer, the only necromancer in many spans, can't raise the dead. Sulien is unsure what his questions are leading to, but feels there's something in it for Marcus. He can't fathom what yet. The tool is worthless. "That's correct."

"Interesting," Marcus says as Carlan stops at the doorway to the hall, his large form darkening the entrance. Marcus's gaze shifts to Carlan.

"You are needed for a moment," Carlan says in his unemotional tone.

Life after Death

Marcus excuses himself. Once he is out of the room, Sulien moves to the table along the wall and pulls the drawer out. There is a single opened tablet of sorts. It has covers on either end, binding in the middle, and the pages are displayed for him to see. Writing scrolls across it as he watches names, dates, times, and locations appear before his eyes in black ink.

Magic, but who or what knows and records when a life will end? He doesn't have time to ponder it as he reads the print, searching for a death becoming of his skills. He doesn't want a battle and, judging by the large number dead at a single location, that's what he's seeing. He continues scrolling with his eyes until he finds one, tomorrow. According to the time it will be morning in Lols. A man fell from his horse two days ago and has suffered alone for the past two days. *That's it*, Sulien thinks and returns to his spot marked with dribbles of blood.

Marcus returns a few moments later. "I apologize for the inconvenience. I'm interested in your tool, making a trade with you. The tool for, say, for metals and stones to create another tool."

Why does he want it? "I'll think on it." Sulien isn't planning a second tool. In the past he used sacrifice, a drop of his own blood or a strand of hair, and always on small animals, never anything as large as a human. He thought it was necessary to use something to amplify the magic, but now thinks it is the sacrifice itself, not the tool. A tool isn't needed.

Mercari's tail feathers greet Leif with a wave as the troll turns. "Come, come."

In a back room of the shop, he points to a smooth jade handle. Just as it was in his vision. Cautiously, as if it might break, Leif touches the handle and runs his finger over the shiny green stone. It is exactly what he saw. He picks it up, impressed with its feel. Mercari tilts his head in expectation and watches Leif. "Its just as I asked."

The troll smiles wide, showing an empty gap in his front teeth. "Excellent," he says and moves toward the other side of the shop, stopping in front of a large canister. "This is the size and dimensions you asked. It is ready, and the filter."

Leif inspects it inside and out, and the filter. There's a layer of fine green sand. Not the sand of the desolate land but the realm with lavender seas. The fae realm. Above that is a layer of shungite, then small, round pebbled rock, more shungite and, on top, larger rocks. It fits like a glove over the canister. "This should work nicely."

Life after Death

Leif takes the pouch with the Iolida and reaches in for one. Mercari stops him. "You don't pay until all is finished. Take the canister and filter and return in two more weeks."

With a nod, Leif places the small bag in his pocket and lifts the canister and filter. It's light enough to carry, although tall enough he can barely see over the top.

Libby and Sisimo are waiting outside as he exits the shop. "You'll never see your way to gran-mo's with that or you'll hit someone on the head. Let me help."

She's probably right. Leif lowers it and they each take a handle hanging from the top. Separated by desert, he feels Sulien's pride swell and his happiness of Sulien's success, then his heart drops a bit as he considers how he'll tell him it is he who will create life from death with the scythe. It is a rune bestowed on him. His mind still reeling in the why, surely Sulien is more skilled. A thought strikes him. One that stabs deep and hard into his heart. Is Sulien alive?

21

ulien noted the similar size in the seed of Serenity Tree and the amber stone as he mashed it with other herbs in mortar and pestle. He didn't think the seed known for its legendary immortal properties would do much good in an ascendant. He scooped the powder into a tincture and closed the lid. Turning to the scroll with his notes, he jotted down the powder and turned to his notes on the ascendant.

A voice inside him warned him to be paranoid, taunted him that, in his absence,

Life after Death

Marcus would send someone to his cave and so he copied the notes for the ascendant, changing the amber stone to a seed from Serenity Tree and burned the old notes. No one but him would know the truth.

Guilt fought its way into his head. He'd always been honest but, in this new world and after speaking with Marcus, he's not sure he can trust anyone except Leif and isn't sure Leif isn't dead in the desert. The sand and winds blowing over his corpse. No, if that was the case Sisimo would return.

In order to beat the harvesters at their job, he decides it's time to join the dying man in Lols. In a few hours he will be gone and the harvesters will send his soul to the afterlife, but not if Sulien beats them to it. Under the light of the double moons, a pink shadow over the desolate land and a silver ball over Aradia, he stands in the sand, places the amber stone inside one half of the ascendant and closes the second half. It clicks under the stone and he says the location and thinks it all at once.

The moons appear to revolve around him as his body spins and suddenly he's staring at a bright reddish ball in the nighttime sky of Lols. Lights twinkle and blink above him. The red moon offers enough light that he sees the man's form lying still in the dirt. He feels they aren't alone, but sees no one. He snaps his fingers, creating a plasma flame on his thumb and shines it over the area.

It lasts only a few minutes in the weakened magic of Lols but long enough to see they are alone. He leans over the man's body and places a hand on his chest. His breathing is weak and his pulse unstable. Thump…thump, thump….thump.

He places a hand under the man's head and lifts. The man's eyes flutter as he attempts to open them. "I've come to help you."

The man's mouth opens but no words come out. His lips are as dry and cracked as the desert of the desolate land and his face is red from the hot daylight ball in the sky. Sulien takes the water bottle he brought and drains some into the man's mouth. "You don't need to say words. Blink once for yes and twice for no."

The man blinks once in understanding.

"Good. I know you are in pain and I can make that pain go away. Do you want that?"

The man blinks once.

"I'm here to give you a gift. A second life. One in which you will achieve immortality and live in a land flowing with nourishment. You will not want or hurt again. Do you accept my gift?"

Life after Death

The man's closed eyes stay closed. He doesn't blink and Sulien thinks maybe he doesn't want it and he'll have to try someone else. When the man's eyes blink, he's relieved. The tool didn't work, the sacrifice didn't work, but never did he ask permission or give the person the choice. Returning life to the dead takes a great sacrifice and he thinks the person must choose to die in order to live.

The man's mouth moves and cracked words exit, "Ki...ll m." It takes so much strain for the man to say those couple choppy words. Sadness wells in his heart, followed with happiness. If he's right and the man wanting death and a second chance is the answer, then he will achieve what he came to the desolate land for.

He presses the tip of the knife into his thumb and drains his blood into the tincture filled with the seed of Serenity Tree and the herbs. He shakes it twice, then takes the knife, centering it over the dying man's heart, closes his eyes and pushes it into his flesh and heart. His ears almost can't take the sound and it's all he hears for a moment.

He pulls the knife out, unable to void his ears of the fleshy sound. His blood runs over his chest and down his ribs. Sulien is used to blood; its stickiness, its metallic odor, and the bright, wet red color. He pours the contents of the tincture over the wound and says, "Death is the end of your first life and the beginning of your second."

The man's finger twitches and Sulien thinks it's only his eyes playing tricks and once again he's unsuccessful, then the man's legs twitch and his body starts convulsing. Out of shock, Sulien jumps to his feet. The man's head falling and smacking the hard packed sand. He steps back several feet, unsure what's happening as the man convulses and twists unnaturally.

The feeling of someone watching and spying returns and he makes another plasma flame. Turning in a circle, he doesn't see anyone or anything, except the packed sand and mountains in the close distance. When he returns to face the man, his eyes widen as they meet him at his level.

The dead man has returned! He finally did it. The man isn't smiling and his eyes shift unnaturally. He opens his mouth wide, as if to bite. Large, pointed canines shine under the moon's light. His mouth opens and closes quickly. His nose wrinkles and he extends a pointed tongue. Fear washes over Sulien's spine, it courses through his blood stream and is the only thing he can hear in his own ears. There's only one thing his body does. On auto-pilot, powered by fight or flight, he runs towards the mountains and the man pursues.

His feet pounding the dirt, his breathing growing ragged, he realizes the mountains are further than they seem. He glances over his shoulder to see the man is chasing, he's on his heel, his mouth open wide and fangs glinting as small beams of light catch them. He searches for something, anything, to hide himself long enough to use the ascendant. This thing he created, whatever it is, he doesn't want to bring it back with him.

It grabs his shirt, tugging him backwards. Sulien reels and spins. Gathering energy in his palms, he uses the only weapon he has and sends a cord of electricity smashing into the man. Its scream is unearthly, deathly, as it echoes through the desert, bouncing off the packed earth and mountains. The electricity sizzles the man's skin and smoke rises from the darkened lash.

When Sulien turns around, he doesn't see the earth fall away beneath him until he drops and rolls downhill. The night spins around him. Stars, sand, and the moon mingle into a blur when his motion stops as the force of his body hits a large stone structure.

He crawls behind the structure, a massive rock of sorts, when his hand sinks into nothing, his face nearly planting in the dirt. He feels and realizes it is an area between the rock and sand. Without hesitation, he squeezes himself into the area before the monster gets up and finishes him off. His body smaller than he ever thought, he hides, keeping his eyes watching.

Footfalls in the sand tell him it's near. He covers his mouth to silence his breathing and can't believe he is hiding from something he made, but it isn't what he thought it would be. The man had a soul and took him only after the man asked, only after he agreed to wanting a second life. He was careful, yet this thing he made is something from a nightmare. More human than the army of the dead raised by the last Marsayan necromancer, but not human enough to live. He knows what he has to do, but doesn't know if he can bring himself to do it.

A howl fills the air, not from his creation, but from something else. A wild animal. It's loud and long, rising and falling in pitch as if calling others or warning them. Sulien reaches into his pocket for the knife. The pocket is empty and he remembers leaving the knife on the ground. He doesn't even have a weapon to kill it. Dirt, dust, paws, and growls tell Sulien the animal and his creation are fighting. Or so he thinks by the sound of the scuffle.

The darkness begins to fade as light turns into day. A screech fills his ears and jolts him to the core. It rings through his body and he knows his creation is dying. A part of him can't stand to hear its suffering and he pulls himself out of the hole, takes a deep breath, and peeks around the side of the rock. It is larger than him. He's never seen anything like it. It is a hill of stone standing alone in a desert.

The creature's screams lessen, and ash blows toward Sulien as its body flames with fire. It licks and eats its flesh away. The sun. Sulien's heart bleeds for the creature, as much as his brain is relieved it's dying. He sees no other body. The animal it fought gone, only large, strange, animal prints remain as the sand washes them away. The prints aren't like any animal he knows; they have a triangular pad surrounded by four smaller oval pads, and deep grooves in the packed earth where its claws tore the ground open remain as the sand washes them away.

REALM WALKER

22

S ulien wrestles in his sleep. The monster he created chasing him through mountains and caves. Glowing stalactites and stalagmites lighting a path sending him deeper into them. Its canines ready to sink into his skin and suck his blood. A cackle breaks up his dream as he runs into a dead-end cavern. A woman in a cloak, dark hair flowing from the sides of the cape, a tattoo like his, two not quite circles chasing each other endlessly. She is a necromancer. Her eyes deep, dark pits and face battered in bottomless wrinkles.

Life after Death

"You can't raise a life with a soul. It is impossible." Her words mock. In her right hand a staff appears. She lifts it to the right and a moving image appears on the cave wall. The dead marching through the colorful land of Marsay. Their skin splotchy and decaying. Their clothing ragged and falling from their shoulders. Pants torn and feet bare. Some are more skeleton than anything living.

"What you seek can't happen. Quit now or raise the long dead."

Sulien stammers. It isn't impossible. Leif saw a vision provided by the visionaries. They don't give false information. "I have seen it."

Her cackle spills into his soul as she vanishes with the final words, "You will try and you will fail."

He wakes with a start, rising immediately and hitting the back of his head against the cave wall. The thump radiates through his skull. He brings a hand to it out of instinct and rubs.

His mind is a flurry as he questions the events. Was the man's soul dark? Is that why he came back as a monster? Was it the seed and herb powder mixed with his blood? In the past he always used a part of him as a sacrifice, but maybe the concoction wasn't needed, added too much or maybe the seed doesn't offer immortality but something much darker. He warned Leif when he collected them, but Leif did it anyways.

He steps outside to the crimson glow that covers the desert and sees Blood River snaking through it. Blood, the life force of the living. The monster wanted to eat, wanted him. Maybe all it needed was blood. In his fear, he ran instead of feeding it. If he'd offered his own blood would it have stopped or sucked him dry?

He decides it's time to bring them to the desolate land. Lols isn't the place. It is filled with violence and death. The desolate land is harsh, not a place of killing but of life.

When Kymani comes by for their weekly journey into Lols, he doesn't mention the man Sulien turned into something not dead but not alive. His time of death, it occurs to Sulien, is the time recorded in Marcus's log. Dawn. That means he was always going to do what he did. He didn't change anything.

The long braid hangs over Kymani's chest and a new growth of stubble covers his chin. He gives no sign that he knows of Sulien's actions, not in his expression or body language, or even tone of voice.

Sulien's other runes, besides the necromancer's mark, give him expertise in all forms of alchemy which served him well in Marsay. This comes to mind as he speaks with Kymani. He doesn't need him or Marcus's log to find the dead. He has crystals and the tools he needs to devise something that will take him to the dying.

He turns Kymani's offer down, saying he is still working on a new tool. Kymani lifts a brow, similar to Leif's trick, then shrugs as if not concerned or even relieved he will be doing his job alone – harvesting the souls who got away. Once he leaves, Sulien gets to work.

He prepares a crystal to seek the dying and a potion to make them sleep. Those aren't the only things he needs as he searches the dune area for more caves and uses vine from Thraves, it grows around the base of the trees and winds their trunks, to weave rope.

Leif holds the finished scythe in his hands. Heady magic flows through it from the jade handle to the iron head and jagged teeth. It connects with him and bonds itself to him. Cold swells through him like an arctic winter. There's no other tool in any realm with magic like that contained in the scythe of immortality. It is his. Whispers purr inside him.

Even after he lays it on the cloth and rolls the cloth around it he can feel its energy. He takes the small cloth satchel from around his waist to pay Mercari for his handiwork.

Realm Walker

The deposit two flowers, the other two are due now.

The troll steps next to him and accepts the payment. His voice low, eyes shifting as if making sure they are alone. "There's one more thing, Drakal." He unfolds a furrowed hand one dramatic finger at a time. Inside his palm rests a ring with a crimson stone made from the Iolida.

Leif's eyebrows drop, he didn't commission a ring. His confused face says more than words.

Mercari doesn't smile, his face stone serious. "The scythe speaks in whispers. Take it." The troll drops it into Leif's hand and closes his fingers around it. "It belongs to the dead."

The troll's words unsettle him as he gathers the supplies to make his return trip. The scythe is powerful enough he doesn't need anything else, such as the seeds of Serenity Tree. Mercari said it speaks. Did it speak to him? Did he spell it with its orders or did the act of smithing it cement its power? Libby explained trolls have a natural tendency with metals and gemstones. Is that it?

More curious is how he called him Drakal. That is the name from his vision. The name he was called. It means death keeper. Is that what he is? He can only imagine the scythe spoke to him, told him that name.

𝕷𝖎𝖋𝖊 𝖆𝖋𝖙𝖊𝖗 𝕯𝖊𝖆𝖙𝖍

The trolls provided plenty of food and water. Carrying more, the return trip will take longer but he'll fare better having plenty of food and water.

"I hope you don't think you're leaving without a goodbye," came Libby's voice from the doorway.

He'd never do such a thing, nor would he ask her to return with him. He lifts his eyes from the satchel he's packing. Every precious moment they'd spent together, he will miss her more now than when they parted in the treacherous lands, but he can't ask her to come. It is a dangerous journey.

Slung over her shoulder are satchels. He gasps, "You have done enough. I don't need more supplies."

"These aren't for you but me. I'm going with you."

Her words bite with pink fluffy joy then melt into anguish. "No, it's too dangerous for me to ask that." He rushes to her and folds her in his arms. "I'll return. It isn't the end."

Her cheek flattens against his chest. "You don't have a choice. We are going with you. You are going to be a father."

Her words startle him. He pushes away far enough to see her face. "A father?"

"Yes. I'm pregnant. We are a family now." Her brown eyes shine with joy and her cheeks flush, not with a bioluminescent glow but pink happiness.

Fizzing bubbles of elation rise like the morning sun. "That's more reason you aren't. It isn't a journey for a mother." Or anyone really, he thinks. "I will take the scythe to Sulien and return for you. We can stay in Verboten." Even as the words leave his mouth he knows it can't be. He is Drakal, the father of those who will live and thrive in the desolate land.

She shrugs his hands away from her shoulders and says, defensively, "I can take care of myself. I've been traveling the treacherous lands all my life. What's a little sand? We can gather food and other necessities from the other realms."

Her words hold so much conviction. How can he deny her? He can't, even though every part of him wants her to stay in Verboten. She will do as Libby does. She takes his hand and presses it to her belly. "Our child needs both of us."

He folds her back into his arms, inhaling her scent, and kisses her head. "I don't have a choice, but promise me if things get rough you will return with Sisimo."

Her head nods against his chest and the word Drakonia echoes through the room on silent wings only he can hear. Its origin the scythe. It speaks. *Blood of my blood, blood of my blood*, recites, growing stronger in his head like the chirps of night insects in chorus.

The large satchel on Sisimo with most of their supplies including the canister and filter. It is light as it hangs from the satchel clinging to a metal chain around one handle. The scythe carried on his back in a scabbard. A satchel around his chest and another around Libby. The three of them leave the land of gemstones and colorful air and head into a land of sand and red skies.

In her bag is a large blanket she says is made of Aradian fabric and stakes she uses to hold the ends to the ground. It isn't much, but shields the three of them from the sands long enough to eat, drink, and sleep. Sisimo has grown much since they left Marsay and makes for plenty of heat in the chilly night as the three of them huddle together under the blanket and stars. Wind and sand whip and pummel their makeshift tent.

Even though they have more to carry, the trip is brighter, happier, not as lonely, and they find moments to laugh. He finds himself thinking often of the child. Will it be so bad? Together they can make a life, find their own cave. There are plenty. With the new filtration system in place they can grow food. His spirits lift each day of the journey and his anticipation grows. In months he will be a father. What will their child be like? A child of

at least three realms, troll, elf, warlock
and…Drakonian?

He asks her as they start their day's
journey, "What do you think of the name
Drakonia?"

She chuckles. "Morbid for a baby."

"Not for the baby. For this land, a real
name instead of the desolate lands or barren
wasteland but a name for this realm; our
home."

She thinks for a moment, her face
deep in concentration. "What does it mean?"

Drakal means keeper of the dead.
That's what the troll, Mercari, called him, and
Drakonia means home of the dead. Not
wanting to tell her that, as she carries life, he
says, "I don't know, but it fits this land. Don't
you think?"

She twists her mouth. "I suppose it
does."

The sands not as relentless this day,
they walk in silence after that. The lowlands
barely visible, they'll make it by nightfall. He
wonders how Sulien has fared in the months
he's been away and imagines his surprise in
the life he brings to the land. Not the life he
will create with the scythe, but the life of his
child.

Libby's belly swollen with child. It
moves inside her. A familiar sadness comes
over him. He doesn't know how Sulien will
react, not only to Libby and the baby, but the

scythe of immortality. It is hem who had the vision. It is he who bears the scythe rune and he who will wield it to bring life to the barren land. He will breathe life from death.

The sand kicks up in the distance, moving in a motion unlike any he's seen. Something is dragging it and, when it stops suddenly, he sees the form of a person and stops cold. It is so far a distance he can't see it clearly, but knows it can see him as the dust cloud moves swiftly towards them.

23

The crystal snaked him through the streets of a city. Its glow brightening as Sulien entered the brick walls. He tucked it into his pocket, afraid it would cause too much attention, but as he lays his eyes on the residents he realizes the entire city is filled with the dead and dying. People with leaky sores, some scabbed over with a black film. He raises his shirt over his nose to curb the smell. His instincts were to heal everyone, but he didn't have the necessary ingredients for curing this many.

Life after Death

His cloak dragged over arms and legs of people as he dodged piles of excrement, legs, arms, and bodies of the sick. It isn't like anything he's ever witnessed.

"Help," a small voice calls. He can't see which dying soul it belongs to. "Help me," it calls again. He scans the piles of people, rows of them deep, leaned against the walls. A hand waves from over a head lumped in an alley. A woman with a man's head in her lap stares at Sulien. Her eyes sinking into his soul. The man's body unmoving. He fears he is already dead.

Deciding he cannot take them all or save them all, he steps over the leg blocking the alley and bends down. "I can help you," he says to the woman.

"And him?" she says, asking about the man.

Sulien studies him, unwilling to soil his hands with the disease they carry. He wraps his finger in the bottom of the sleeve of his cloak and presses against the man's neck. There, yes, barely, but there is a pulse. The man is alive but won't be much longer, nor does he feel the woman will be. "Yes, I can help both of you, but you must agree to leave this place for another flowing with a single resource that carries the essence of life. It is there I can help you."

"Take us," she says with labored breath.

Realm Walker

Sulien pulls the needle made from the thumper and filled with a serum to make them sleep. "This will reduce the pain," he says as he pushes it into the man's neck. When she doesn't fight, he takes a second needle and pushes it into her neck. She wears a simple chain. He lifts it from her chest as she drifts to sleep. A cross dangles from it. He lowers his face to her chest and her eyes flutter and close. He doesn't worry about what people might think or rumors they might spread as he clicks the ascendant in place.

No stories will spread, as every one of them will be dead in days. The air spins until dizziness overwhelms him then dissipates in the cave he made for them. He binds their arms and ankles, feeling silly, but remembers the man dying in the desert and feels it is better not to take chances.

As he gathers blood from the river, he wonders if Marcus's log will include the man and woman in his cave or if they've vanished from the page. By the time he returns, the man's pulse is so weak he isn't sure he didn't miss his window of death, but then a light thump against his finger tells him he is still alive, barely. His skin is cold and sweaty with fever.

He lays the crystal on the floor and waits. It will tell him when death occurs. He hopes it happens before either wake, but has more sleep serum and needles ready if it doesn't.

Within a few hours, the crystal glows red and the man breathes his last. He never gained his permission as he was a step away from death when he found him. Sulien takes the blood and pours it into a chalice of his design. It bears the necromancer's symbol. He opens the man's mouth and says in warlock, "Death isn't the end of your life, but the beginning. In death you shall live off the essence of life."

Lifting the chalice to the man's mouth, he pours the blood. It runs over the man's tongue and begins to spill from the sides, running over his cheeks and dropping to the floor. Sulien closes the man's mouth and places a hand over it.

He isn't at all sure what to expect and waits in a side cave with the cloak over his head to shield his eyes in case the man wakes. Nothing appears to happen, but the crystal changes color, going from red to yellow. Yellow indicating illness. It no longer registers the man.

After some time, the woman stirs. He crawls out from the hidden cave and sticks another thumper needle filled with serum into her neck. He thinks to check the man. Remembering the man in the desert had long, pointed canines, he chooses his wrist instead of neck. A steady rhythm, strong and healthy, thumps against his finger. His lips rise in a smile. He did it. If only the man would wake. He won't rush it and will wait it out. Life is a fragile pursuit.

When his stomach growls, he doesn't rush to his own cave but stays until the pains of hunger are so strong he can't push them away. Day and night and day and night has fallen again when he leaves the cave.

He doesn't eat much, swallowing a glass of water and stuffing dried fruit into his mouth. He takes more dried fruit with him and eats it while he gathers more blood. Fresh blood from the river. Returning to the cave, he pauses before entering. Noise filters into his ears. He ducks his head below the archway and sees the man's head moving. It whips quickly when Sulien enters and, for the first time, his eyes are open. They are brown. The sores covering his body are gone.

He isn't only alive but healed. The man's brows lower as he spots the woman on the floor. He studies her, but doesn't seem to recognize her. Sulien pours the fresh blood into a cup, not the chalice. "You must be thirsty," he says, carefully placing the glass in the man's hands. His wrists are tied but his hands are free.

The man doesn't say anything, but wraps his fingers around the glass and lowers his head and sniffs. The scent triggers something as he lifts it to his mouth and drinks, more flowing over his shirt than making it down his throat.

"I'm Sulien. I found both of you almost dead and brought you here. I am an alchemist and a necromancer. Can you tell me anything about you?"

The man's nose wrinkles, his eyes studying Sulien's face. There's something about the action that reminds Sulien of the man in the desert. He can't place it exactly, and his mind envisions the man's fangs then sees his body sizzling under the electric bolt. He wiggles his feet then, kicks his legs bound at the ankles.

"That is a precaution for my safety and yours. Outside here is safe for you, but not beyond the red sky. There it isn't safe," he says, remembering how the sun killed his last experiment. He burst into flames, his ash spreading over the hard desert ground.

The man stays quiet and Sulien wonders if he can talk. Unsure what to do, he sits across from the man in the cave. Time passes as the bright red daylight sky turns to the crimson evening sky. The crystal flashes red and he knows the woman is passing into death.

He scoots to her side, on the opposite side of the man. His eyes study Sulien as he opens her mouth and pours blood from the chalice down her throat and recites the spell in warlock. The man's head cocks as if in recognition of something. The words maybe.

He expects the woman won't wake for a couple days, so he fills the glass once more with blood and gives it to the man who drinks, making less of a mess. Maybe they are like children and will have to relearn everything. Sulien leaves them and settles in his own cave for the night.

When he returns in the morning, he gasps to see they are gone. How? They were bound. Their ropes laying on the floor of the cave. Had the woman woken? It took the man two days to wake. A shiver spreads over his body in a ripple.

The person moves with unnatural speed, causing the sand to appear as if in wind. It isn't natural or normal, and Leif knows little of other subspecies. What he does know doesn't make him think it's a fae or elf but something else, something dangerous. "Quick, climb onto Sisimo's back," Leif says as he puts pressure on Sisimo's hind legs to sit and slides the satchel off.

"What is that?" Libby asks.

"I don't know, but in the air you are safe from it," he says, practically lifting her

Life after Death

onto Sisimo's back. "He is strong and will take you somewhere safe."

Libby leans over and takes a hold of Leif's shoulder, holding a clump of the cloth from his cloak in her hand. "Not without you. He can carry us both."

It's close, almost on them. There isn't time and he can't risk Libby and the child. "No. Go!"

Sisimo takes wing and Libby's grasp releases. Leif has no weapons, but he has his runes. The magic isn't as strong, but his will is, and the scythe on his back powers him to take the risk and push wind toward the fast moving creature. Sand covers it and seems to disorient it, but doesn't stop it. It is close, close enough to see it is a woman. Blood courses from her mouth, sharp fangs protrude over her lips. Her blonde hair is filthy and her clothing soiled from dirt, not sand. *What did you do, Sulien?*

It isn't natural. Her eyes lock to his and a voice whispers in his ear: *She isn't life, but the embodiment of death. Use your plasma.*

The scythe's words clear in his head, and with it on his back, he conjures plasma. It is the first rune. A magic fundamental to all warlocks. He lets go of a beam that strikes the woman and wraps her legs. She screams and smoke pours from her leg as if the plasma burns her. He pulls it back and forms it into a sword. It glows blue from the magic. While she is down and in pain, he thrusts the sword into her heart.

Flames burst from her chest and lick the air as they travel over her body. She wriggles and turns, a rush of flame bursts from the air. From Sisimo. Griffons only use their fire in defense.

The fire consumes her body until all that is left is ash. The wind, as if on purpose, carries the ash in a gust, mixing it with the desert sands away from him, towards the midland range.

Life after Death

24

Rushing out of the cave, Sulien scans for either of them and spots prints from bare feet heading towards the river. He follows, not sure what he'll do if he finds them, not sure what he'll do if he doesn't. They can't leave the desolate land. The sun is too bright in the other realms, but are these new creations similar to the man in the desert?

The man leans on his hands and knees over the flowing river, as if it's impossible to drink too much of the sticky red liquid. He turns his head when he sees Sulien, stands abruptly and runs away, his feet splashing through the blood of the river, heading towards the falls. His speed faster than anything Sulien has ever seen in his life. In that moment, he's impressed and wonders what other magic the creature acquired in death.

Sulien runs after him. He will be trapped or die if he tries to pass through the falls. "I can help you," he calls, but the man's unreal speed takes him quickly away. His agile feet carry him closer to the falls. "Stop!" But his words fall on empty air. The man no longer in Sulien's vision.

He continues, and shivers erupt over his skin and a wave of heat courses through him. Sweat trickles his forehead and the cloak stifles him. He pushes forward until he spots the man standing at the falls.

"I can help you," he says, out of breath, body bent, and hands pressed on his knees.

The man turns his dark eyes and fix on Sulien. They are pained. He can see that even from the distance between them. Sulien moves closer and the man steps back as if Sulien is…plagued, like the man and the woman when he found them.

More shivers crawl over his skin and he realizes he has what they died from. It will take him too and he won't return.

Life after Death

The man drops, a long, wooden rod jutting from his back. He falls to his hands and knees. Shrieks of pain bellow from his mouth. On the cliff beside the falls stands a man. A harvester. His long braid falling over his chest. Kymani.

Sulien's gaze flicks to the man in the river. He rushes to him. Black poison pumps through the veins in his arms and neck. "No!"

His screams follow him as he joins the man in the river, blood soaking through his pants. "You killed him," he shouts upwards towards Kymani. "Why?"

Kymani's words sail down, "He was a monster, like the one you created in Lols. While you were hiding under a rock, I was watching."

The memories of that night and the thing he created sail through his head and sink in his heart. Tears fill his eyes.

"It fought a wolf. A human wolf, not a lycan, but a human man. The wolf man's bite slowed it down. If the sun hadn't killed it the bite would have."

Kymani's voice is closer and Sulien tilts his head backwards to see him coming down the mountain, using the rocks as steps.

"He...this one wasn't like that," he says through his sadness. His voice cracking.

"He was. He tried to enter Thraves, but the sun burned his hand and he pulled back. Life isn't meant to be returned once it is taken. When night fell and the sun no longer kept him here, he would leave this place and feed on innocents. Fill the realms with death."

No! No! No! Sulien shakes his head, but knows his words are true. There is one more out there he must find before she is able to leave. The weight of failure burrows inside him. "Stop!" he calls. He doesn't want to tell him he is plagued, nor that a woman is still out there. "I'll take his body and burn it and you don't ever need return."

"I wasn't planning on joining you," Kymani says from about mid height of the falls. A quiver filled with arrows hits a rock a few feet from Sulien. "Take them. They are soaked in lycan blood. Don't worry, I have more."

Sulien stands, chills running the course of his body as it's taken with fever. He grabs the quiver, turns on his heel to do what must be done.

Life after Death

25

eif gives in to Libby, and Sisimo carries them to the treacherous lands. He knows he will not stay. He cannot stay. He smooths Libby's hair as she lays her head on his lap.

The tiny red Iolida shine in bunches and he looks at his ring. It doesn't shine, but sparkles under the lights in the sky when they catch it just right.

Mercari took the seed from one of the flowers and fashioned a ring. He understood, on some level, the magic contained in the scythe. It spoke to him.

Will it speak to him when the time is right? It leans against a tree, still swathed in cloth. *Why him?*

He leans and moves his hand to Libby's resting on her large belly. It won't be long now and he hopes he can return before the baby is born.

She smiles at him. Her eyes studying the line of his chin. "I hope the baby has your spirit," she says.

"I hope the baby has your ingenuity."

"That's it!" she says, her body glowing for a moment. Not bright, but subtle enough it can't be missed.

"Maybe the baby will glow like you."

"I hope not." She chuckles and places a hand over his on her belly.

He lowers her head gently to a bed of leaves and curls next to her. Sisimo in a large ball at her feet.

He holds her until she's asleep, then sets off for Drakonia. Sisimo will take care of her.

Sulien drags the man's body on the dry rocks and leaves him to go in search of the woman. His body wracked in chills, he doesn't know how long he has before the

Life after Death

more debilitating symptoms hit him. There's no time.

Out of breath, he follows the river, hoping she stayed close to blood. He was foolish in his endeavors. This was never his journey. Leif should have let him die at the pyre.

He finds no sign of her and stops. His body cold and hot with fever. His lymph nodes swollen like round fruit. *How long before necrosis?* he thinks, remembering the black, pus-filled and leaking sores on their bodies.

Unable to move further, he lays on the ground, not caring how much sand fills his hair and clothes. A wind rushes over him, dumping desert sand onto him. Each tiny grain nothing remarkable, but with all the trillions of sand particles, a massive desert.

Did life ever exist in this land? Before the harvesters drained the blood of the dead into the land? Maybe many spans past before the great collision that created the middle and outer realms. In his many months in the desert, he'd seen no sign life ever existed. No animal shells or insect exoskeletons, no fossil structures embedded in the cave rock. Nothing. No life.

Mixed in with the sand is something heavier than the largest pebble of sand, yet not bulky enough to be a rock. It hits his ribs and slides off, dropping to the ground near his side with a barely audible clink. He reaches his hand and feels metal. The object catches on his finger and he brings it to his face.

Lacking energy, it feels like it's heavy as he lifts his hand and studies it. It's a chain with a cross. The woman! It's hers. With a burst of energy he sits up and notices he isn't covered in sand but ash.

She's gone. He laid in her ashes. Fever sends waves of torment over his large body. He shivers.

Blue flames descend from the sky and scorch and char the ground. Heat plumes against Sulien's body. He doesn't know if it's the flames or the fever. A low voice says, "Did you think you could hide your intentions?"

The body of a massive, winged animal transforms into a large man with red, wavy hair resembling flames on his head. So red it flashes in fire and simmers. He seems real as the heat eddies over Sulien's body, but his brain is delusional and heady with fever. "I wasn't hiding anything."

"Don't lie!" The man's words shake the ground.

"I should burn you where you are, but I'll let your sickness take you. You deserve no less than a miserable death."

The man's body transforms into an animal. Its wingspan is enormous as it takes wing into the night.

26

Leif makes it to the cave only to find it empty. Propped near the filter and blood puddle is a scythe with a pearl handle and head from driftwood. The driftwood branch Sulien salvaged from the lake of faces. He almost died, could have died, but he didn't. He said, 'I'm tougher than the lake'. He doesn't touch the scythe but studies it with a probing eye.

There's a small metal device in Sulien's work area. It's made of metal and shaped like a gear. It fits comfortably in his hand. There are two identical halves. He doesn't know what it does and replaces it where he found it. There isn't time to study the scrolls. Several are rolled near the work area. He's sure the answers are in them, but his focus is finding Sulien. Sulien could be dead or gone or dying.

The lowlands grow, each hill taller than the last. The river cuts a path through them. He looks towards the falls. "Sulien," he calls, with no response.

Heading towards the falls, he calls his name again. No response. Guts twist like hands wringing a rag. They know Sulien isn't OK. He's not just out for a walk or even visiting their neighbors in Thraves or digging for a rock that can be fashioned into a tool for necromancy. His gut says he needs to move quick. Running, he doesn't stop. His boots hit the ground, dust flies and swirls around him. The rock near the falls is black, charred from fire. His heart thumps with the beat of his feet within his chest.

"Sulien." He drops to his knees on the dusty rock. Ash swirls in the sand around him, reminding him of the woman. His plasma burned her, then Sisimo scorched her, leaving nothing but ash on the wind. No, this isn't Sulien. It's another he created. He stands and takes a step back. This can't be Sulien.

Running, he follows the river until he finds glass in the sand. Its shine draws him close and he sees him. Sulien lying in the sand, his cloak ripped to shreds and charred at the edges. Where did the fire come from? Did Sulien use fire to destroy more of the … things he created? How many?

Leif drops to his knees beside Sulien. Sand pebbles are embedded in his long hair and beard. Dangling from his hand is a silver chain.

"Sulien," he calls and the man doesn't stir. Taking his cloak off, he rolls Sulien onto it and drags him to the cave. He rolls him off his cloak in Sulien's room and begins to strip the tattered clothing from the man when he notices his swollen lymph nodes. His body is cold with fever.

In the alchemy lab, he mixes a serum and a salve using the herbs and materials he brought from Marsay. He knows enough, but Libby knows more. He takes another look at Sulien and decides against involving Libby. Yes, she might be able to save him, or she might not. It would be too risky. The illness could be contagious, and she is with his child and he… The thought settles in his head, its weight crushing him. By proximity, he may have the illness too.

He hasn't touched his flesh or the swollen nodes. He won't. He takes a thumper syringe and carefully fills it with the serum that he injects into Sulien's exposed arm. It's inflamed from the sand beating on it, brushing over it like sandpaper. He rips the cloth from his own shirt and coils it tight. He uses that to apply the salve. There's nothing more he can do until Sulien wakes.

Torn, he wants to stay but knows he should leave. The longer he is near him, the more chance he has of contracting the illness. Sulien's cavern room where he lays is only one room. He considers if the larger area is safe, and decides it's better to stay out of the cave. He slips outside and rests along the sandy bank. It is a compromise.

The next day, he rips another piece of cloth from his sleeve and uses it to cover his mouth and nose, then enters the cave. A black sore has formed on Sulien's cheek. Necrosis. His flesh is dying. *What did you do to bring a plague on yourself?*

The following day breaks before Sulien stirs. Excitement fills Leif as he jumps to his feet and darkens the doorway. He is shocked to see a man with a long, dark braid and a weapon on his back. No, not a weapon, but a scythe. Its head made from red rock He shuffles through Sulien's scrolls.

"What are you doing? Those aren't yours," Leif says, his voice loud enough to be heard, but not yelling. The man is close to his size; tall and muscular.

Hearing his voice, the man turns, a couple scrolls under his arm. Leif yanks them and they spill to the floor. "You must be the absent assistant," the man says in a cocky voice.

Leif doesn't like his tone or the self-assured twist of his lip. "I am…not absent any longer."

"Sulien," the man says, as his eyes roam the large cavern. "In your absence has done things he shouldn't. He went to the outer realm without me. The first time, he made a monster. The second time, he returned with a monster. I killed it."

Monster. Like the one with unnatural speed that Leif killed in the desert. There was more than one? The idea sinks into Leif's belly and churns. It was a guess. The glassy sand and charred rock were clues, but he didn't think there were more. Not really. Sulien made horrible decisions in his absence, but he is still the closest thing Leif has to a father. He is the man who raised him and taught him alchemy. "You should leave. Sulien is ill, deathly ill."

The man tilts his head toward the smaller cavern Sulien rests in. "Yes, he cursed himself."

No, he didn't! Leif's mind snaps a little too quickly as the thought crossed his mind too. An illness that causes necrosis to a necromancer… He steadies his thoughts, not willing to agree with the man. There is a more probable explanation. He went to the outer realm and exposed himself to a deathly disease.

Leif says none of that. Sulien is Leif's business and he will use everything he knows to save him. If it's possible, he will find a way. "What do you want?"

"The tool he used to portal," the man says, his demeanor cool and distrusting, his long frame at full height and shoulders square.

"Take it!" Leif hears his voice rise an octave. This man has no business here.

"I would if I knew which of these items it is." The man's eyes rest on the tools of Sulien's trade.

Leif picks up the fallen scrolls and throws them at him. "Take them all and leave. I will give you the tool when you can identify which one it is."

The scrolls hit the man in his chest and drop to his feet. He doesn't move a muscle as he studies Leif.

"Leif," a weak voice carries through the cave. Sulien.

Life after Death

27

Two voices argue in his head. The sound is long, stretched bands of color. He doesn't understand anything of what they've said. They grow louder and his eyes open to a fuzzy world. After blinking several times, the room comes into and out of focus. It is the cavern. His eyes fall on the pearl-handled scythe and he remembers it didn't work.

Nothing worked. Thoughts stream through his head, faraway images with ambiguous edges. Blue fire scorching the ground and people. The thoughts swim as they attempt to manifest in his conscious mind. The voices return in sharp focus. Leif. Is it the illness toying with him? Is anything real?

The voice sounds again and he calls, "Leif." His words croaked with pain and his throat dry. They barely squeak, but he hasn't the energy to try again.

A shadow darkens the doorway, and a head of hair falls over his shoulders. His shirt is ripped and a cloth covers his nose and mouth and a plume of hair hangs beneath. It is his eyes that Sulien knows. They are dark pools of worry.

"Sulien," he says as he stands in the doorway. One hand pressed against the inside of the larger cavern then he disappears and Sulien thinks he is delusional. Surely, his body is still in the sand and ash. He is dead and this is his afterlife, but the man returns and moves closer.

No, he can't remember why at first, not until the man is beside him with a glass of clear liquid. It is the liquid for the living not the dead. Blood is the liquid of the dead. A silver band with a blood-red stone is on his finger. Is that something the trolls gave him?

Sulien tries to lift his arm but it doesn't move. The man's fingers move under Sulien. They are soft, like fabric. He lifts his hand and dribbles water over Sulien's mouth.

𝕷𝖎𝖋𝖊 𝖆𝖋𝖙𝖊𝖗 𝕯𝖊𝖆𝖙𝖍

He stretches his cottony tongue outward and catches a drop, then another, and more.

Slowly the water wets his throat and the incoherent thoughts become solidified. This isn't his death. It is a plague he brought to himself. It is the source punishing him for returning human life. For making monsters like the last necromancer, a woman who made an army of the dead. His creations not an army, but not exactly living either.

Images of fire flash behind his eyes. They burned to death because of him. Did their souls move to the afterlife or will they roam the realms forever, haunted, angry, and lonely? "You returned," he says, the words crack as his mouth forces them out.

"I did. Tell me how to help you?" His voice is sincere and distress blooms in his tone. It isn't the joyous one he expected after his journey.

"You can't… It is my...penance." Each words a struggle. He is weak.

Leif's eyebrows lower and in his eyes flash answers, followed by darkness. "My trip was a success, but everything is in the desert. I'll go back for it when you are better. Tell me what I need to mix and what spells to perform."

"What aren't…you saying?"

Leif's eyes drop and shift. He sets the glass on the floor, brings his hand to his shirt and lowers it over his collarbone. A rune in the form of a scythe with jagged teeth. It is larger than most runes.

He feels his lips curve at the ends. Of course, Sulien is dying, he will not bring life back from death. It was never him, always Leif. "I have to tell you…everything."

"No." Leif shakes his head, his eyes staying too long on the doorway. He brings his knees up. "I don't need to know."

Or you don't want to know, but you need to. All the mistakes Sulien; made Leif can't repeat them. "Yes, you need to understand."

Leif glances over his shoulder again as if something is in the cavern. Sisimo maybe, but why does he keep watching as if nervous or distrusting of something. "Later, when you have strength. Rest. I'll bring more water. You passed out in the desert and are dehydrated." He dips a swath of fabric into a bowl and brings it to Sulien's neck and dabs.

He remembers the voices. Was he talking to Sisimo? The salve is cool and tingles. He fiddles with something beside him. Sulien can't see, but knows when he raises it what it is. A serum in a needle. He presses it into Sulien's bare arm.

The room swims and everything goes out of focus until Sulien drifts into nothingness.

Life after Death

The man sits on the floor and reads the scrolls. They are all piled to his side. "I told you to leave," Leif says with authority.

"And I told you I will when I have the device." He doesn't look up from the print when he says it. "What language is this?"

That's right. He isn't a warlock and can't read the words. "One you don't know."

The man drops the scroll into his lap. "But you do."

"I'm not literate," Leif says and steps outside, lowering the mask. He glances towards the treacherous lands and thinks of Libby. Her soft hair plays against his hand in phantom feels, her laughter fills his ears, and the kick of his child pushes against the palm of his hand.

He doesn't know how long he has before he, too, starts showing signs of illness. His thoughts reverting to the man. He can stay, breathe the air and inhale the disease. No, he doesn't really want him to die. It is his anger and hopelessness speaking.

A dark form takes wing over the treacherous lands and his gut clenches like a clamp. Sisimo! Leif drops to his knees. Libby! She's stubborn and independent. In his heart he knows Sisimo isn't alone. She's with him.

Realm Walker

No! No! It is the perfect storm. All the elements in Leif's life spinning out of control as they culminate at one central point and he's powerless to stop it.

He will insist she return to the treacherous lands or Verboten. Anywhere but here. She and the baby can't be exposed to the illness.

.

28

As the shadow grows closer his worst fears are confirmed. He waves his arms and pushes them forward to show they should return, but the griffon stays on course. He runs toward them, waving frantically for them to go. His efforts are worthless. When Sisimo lands, Leif runs to his side. "Go back, return. It isn't safe here."

Libby takes in a strained lungful of air. "The baby is…coming," she says through broken breaths.

Realm Walker

"You can't have the baby here! Sulen is ill, deathly ill!" He hears the panic in his voice.

Libby isn't moved by it. She stands firm. "The baby isn't…waiting!" she says as she pulls her leg over Sisimo to slide down.

He can catch her or let her fall. It isn't a choice. He raises his arms and catches her as she slips to the ground. Her round belly rubbing against Leif. "Please stay out here, at least."

"I'm part elf, I can he—" she starts to say. Her words cut off by a strong contraction as she squeezes her eyes closed. He collects her in his arms and carries her to the outside wall of the hill. "I'll bring you whatever you need. Just tell me."

"Take me inside," she orders.
"No!"

She squirms in his grasp. Her stubbornness may kill her and the baby, maybe he already has. Holding her in his arms after exposure to the disease may be all it needs to incubate inside her. His room is on the other side of the main cavern. If he takes her there, she will be as far from Sulien as possible inside the cave.

"Who are you?" she asks as they enter the large cavern. Her voice tense, not from suspicion but labor. Leif, in his frenzy, forgot all about the man searching through the scrolls.

Life after Death

"Kymani," he says and opens his mouth as if to say something else. Instead he closes it as Sisimo enters the cave and gives the griffon a narrow-eyed glance. Not one of alarm, but curiosity.

He carries Libby past Kymani, ignoring him, and lays her down on his makeshift bed. It isn't much more than a couple blankets. This isn't the way he wanted his baby to be born. In Verboten, on a proper bed with proper linens, but she chose this. Why, he doesn't know. Even the brass forest floor in the treacherous lands would be 100% better than this. A cave of illness and death.

While he smooths the blankets and sits down, clasping her hand in his, she gives him a verbal list that includes water. Water, there's never much here, but she hasn't been to the lands. She doesn't know. The filter he left in the desert is because they lack water, or at least the amounts they need to sustain life.

As he pulls his legs to stand she squeezes his hand, he meets her gaze as she says, "In death is life and life is death."

He leans down and kisses her head. If he can help it, all will live.

When he returns to the large inner cavern he halts and looks Kymani square in the eyes. They are roughly the same size. Kymani is no more than five feet from him. He wants an ascendant and has shown he isn't leaving without it.

REALM WALKER

Leif ducks and leans down over the alchemy station and grabs the device. He knows what it is without reading a single scroll. When he left, the item didn't exist, neither did the pearl-handled scythe. It could only be one of the two and the process of elimination leaves only the two halves of the ascendant. He leans down and collects half and pushes the other half behind a mixing bowl. "Here, take it!" he says, thrusting his hand towards the man.

Kymani's long braid falls over his arm when he leans down to collect it. Flipping it in his hand, he studies it. "There's more. It looks like a seed fits here." He points to a half an oval shape.

Leif wants him gone. He has a baby on the way and a dying man to care for. Scanning the items, he sees the seeds from Serenity and grabs one. It looks roughly the right size. "Take it!" he says, standing. He is out of time. Libby's breathing and pains reaching his ears.

The man puts the seed over the indent and nods. He turns, then stops. This catches Leif's attention, as he assumed he'd finally leave, but when he looks through the cave opening he sees it. Rain, but not any rain. The sky is raining blood.

The man turns and faces Leif. "What can I do to help?"

𝕷𝖎𝖋𝖊 𝖆𝖋𝖙𝖊𝖗 𝕯𝖊𝖆𝖙𝖍

Leif isn't fooled the man wants to help, but at the moment he could use it. He points towards the empty cavern with the small filter they rigged and hands him a bowl. "Go through there and fill this with water. Empty the filtration canister and return it so it can filter more water."

The man takes the bowl and stoops as he enters the room. Leif collects everything else Libby asked for and joins her. Her legs spread, a blanket over them, she breathes hard and stifles her screams. He can't take away the pain but he can comfort her, sit by her, ask if he can do anything else.

"No! It won't…be…long!" she says, the words coming out as a broken scream.

It pains him to see her go through this. He's never witnessed a birth. Her back is against the wall, knees in the air, as Kymani enters with the water. "He's calling for you."

Leif takes a glance at Libby, then Kymani. "Stay with her." He ducks out of the cavern and into Sulien's. He looks worse than he did earlier. The salve doesn't appear to work, as another black blister forms on his arm. His nodes just as large as they were.

Sulien's gaze locks on Leif. "Let me be the first." He pauses and gulps a breath. "That is my purpose just as yours… is to use that scythe to bring life… to this desolate land."

Realm Walker

Leif sits on the floor beside him. "No, I can't. You're going to be fine."

"No, I'm dying. Give me…this dignity." With force Leif doesn't expect, probably all Sulien has left, he reaches for Leif's shirt and catches the bottom in his hand. "Turn me."

The idea makes Leif's skin crawl. How can he turn the man who raised him? The only father he knows. The man who is a shell of who he was. His large frame reduced to a mottled, black blistered mess. Would it be worse to allow him to keep living this life or give him a second chance?

Is it worse to use the scythe on him or let him die this excruciating death? He decides the death is worse, nods solemnly, and ducks out of the cavern.

The scythe is wrapped and lying against the wall inside the large cavern. Under the blanket, it doesn't look like anything special. The jade handle and iron head with its jagged teeth are hidden. He lowers it and unrolls the blanket. He remembers how cold ice moved through him when he held it.

Sisimo's tail hangs out of the cavern room that is his. The one Libby is in. The one his baby will enter the world in. He picks up the scythe. Its power courses through him with frost, settling inside his bones. It whispers words he can't make out. Whispers cover whispers, as if a thousand people are whispering at one time.

The image of Libby, back to the wall, pushing their child into the world without him, hurts like a well of sadness. Her sweet face working to hide her painful grimace. It rips his heart to make the choice between her and Sulien, between Sulien's first life and using the scythe to give him a second life. He doesn't fear the scythe won't work. He saw the vision. He fears what Sulien might become. One of those like the monsters Sulien created.

The hisses of the room murmur like bug wings rubbing against one another until they reach a pinnacle and all Leif hears is: *It is time*. Libby was right, in life is death. In death is life.

Sulien wheezes as Leif enters his cavern. Its red and gold striped walls a sight he wishes he'd never seen. The place they both called home for months before the journey to Verboten that changed everything. Kneeling at his side, a hand under Sulien's head, his salt and pepper hair, now more salt than pepper and filled with sand, sweeps over the hardened sand-rock floor. He painfully turns his head as Sulien grows weaker and weaker and the baby stronger and stronger as if it is sucking his life force.

A new life for an old one. It isn't the end for his mentor, but a new beginning. A second life. 'In death is life and life is death.' Libby's words echo in his mind.

Sulien's eyes close and his lips part, sound spilling into the air around them. "Make me the first." His words are so quiet, yet loud in Leif's ears.

He swallows, the scythe in his hand. Its jade handle cool and radiating magic. When he raises it, the ring on his finger fashioned by Mercari shines red light. Its soft glow radiates through the cavern. Tears well in his eyes. Libby's screams fill his ears. The jade handle firm in his grasp he says, "Life in death and death in life." The words aren't practiced, but find their way from deep inside him, echoing through the scythe of immortality, and with a painful swallow of spit he drives the teeth of the scythe into Sulien's chest.

White light streams upwards in blinding bands, erupting through the cavern system and into the crimson sky, and his ring returns to normal. His mind reminded of Libby as her wails pierce his ears. The scythe still in his hand, he runs to her and drops to his knees. A tiny, wiggling, blood-coated baby lies over her chest.

Kymani stares, wide eyed and mouthed, as if he too has never witnessed birth.

The sandy floor beneath her is coated in blood. "No!" he screams again and again.

Life after Death

"Libby!" Her lack of response, the stillness of her chest, crashes into his. The tiny red baby screams, reminding him of new life. He cradles the tiny baby in his arms, presses his cheek gently against its head. This is all he has of her.

"I'm sorry," a male voice filters through the baby's screams into Leif's head as he turns to Kymani. "I did everything she asked. I couldn't stop the bleeding."

Leif wants to blame him, curse at him, but he can't. It isn't his fault. The baby's life for hers and Sulien's. It is the price. With strong magic comes sacrifice.

"She's gone. They are both gone." His face a mess of tears.

"She is, but I can give you a moment alone before her soul passes. I need the scythe Sulien made."

Leif is too distraught to question him and points him to Sulien's cavern. "It's with him." Sisimo's bushy tail sweeps across the floor and rests on Libby's legs.

The man nods, leaves, and returns with the pearl-handled scythe. He empties something from a bag into his palm. Rocks. They clink against each other. He places them in various spots, forming a circle around her body, then takes the red-headed scythe off his back. A blue light bounces off the head. It zaps as he balances the scythe and reaches for the other. The one with the pearl handle.

Realm Walker

Leif admires his strength as he holds both scythes. One in each hand. The blue light attaches and stretches to the driftwood head. Warmth and love fill his heart. It's beautiful. Kymani moves the scythe upwards and slowly, as if it is an art, and drags a translucent form out of it.

It isn't any form but Libby.

"I'm sorry," he weeps, the wiggling baby finally calm in his arms.

"He's perfect, isn't he?" she says. She isn't in any pain as she looks on her child with love. Her form glows as she does when she's excited.

Leif hasn't even thought of the child's gender until that moment. He agrees with a nod, wanting to take her in his arms, but he's afraid she'll pop like a bubble.

"Take me, too, before it's too late." Her eyes plead along with her words. How does she know? In the pangs of birth, was she paying attention to him? No, she heard his thoughts.

Who is he to deny her and how long does she have before her next home claims her? He brings the child to Sisimo who pushes out his front legs and rests the baby on them. Returning to her body, he raises the scythe. A crimson glow fills the room from the ring on his finger. It spreads over the room, as it did with Sulien. It is right, he feels it, as the scythe sends a wave of cold rushing

Life after Death

through him. He drives the teeth into her chest, doing as she asked. "Life from death and death in life," he says. Her translucent form loses its shape as light spills upwards and outwards.

When it dissipates, spots fill his eyes. "Thank you," he says to Kymani. He isn't sure, but thinks a tear runs down the man's cheek before he belts a bloodcurdling scream.

Leif's eyes grow wide as the spots clear and a form fills the space behind Kymani. He recognizes the eyes, but they aren't the eyes he knew. They look like them but different and saturated with darkness and red lines fill the whites. His canines extend over his bottom lips as he licks the blood drops on them.

A finger traces the edges of his neck. He jumps to the side. Libby leaps toward him, tripping over Sisimo's tail as he whips it in her path. A bundle in the griffon's beak. There is only one thing he can do. The creatures he made want Kymani and maybe him. They want their blood. He thrusts the only weapon he has into Kymani's chest and screams to Sisimo, "Take him somewhere safe," while using the blinding light to push past Sulien and into the desert.

Sisimo takes wing, rising into the air and west toward Verboten. Leif doesn't look back as he runs. If they follow, and he wants

184

them to, he won't stop, can't stop, until the baby is safe.

In his vision from the visionaries, the creatures were fast. In life they are fast too, as claws dig into his flesh, pulling him down. He rolls to his back as three sets of sharp, canine fangs dig into his flesh and the shadow of wings spread high into the sky. The baby is safe.

Only the purest of souls can wield me... carries on the wind. Its words bringing a revelation. He understands the power of sacrifice. It isn't Sulien's death, or Libby's, but his, so they can live. He must die so they may endure. An entire species of undead to fill the desolate land he calls Drakonia. It was always his destiny. He is Drakal – father of the dead. His sacrifice will pass to his descendants. So long as one exists, so will the undead in Drakonia. Their lives inexplicably tied together and they will pay greatly. The thought dissipates as he falls into his final sleep of death.

29

Julien looks at Leif's lifeless body drained of blood. Libby whimpers at the loss of the man she cared so deeply for she birthed his child. Her loss is double, as her child is gone too. She understands it's better that way, as she can't be a proper mother to it, but that doesn't take the pain away.

Kymani appears dazed. The slits in his eyes lessen as the blood rain stops and the shielded, desolate land sun returns. "We need to bury him."

Realm Walker

He is right. It is their shame. Sulien's guilt rests like a weighty gold brick on his shoulders. Leif trusted him and loved him, but will never carry the name father of the ...*vampires* Sulien decides.

It was their lust for blood that killed Leif and in his sacrifice they can live. Sulien finally understands why his creations didn't work and why they ran from him. When a vampire first turns, it craves fresh, pumping blood. It sees the living heart, smells its blood, and can think of nothing else until the thirst is quenched. It also knows unhealthy blood tainted by sickness. They quickly learn not to drink straight from the river but in the underground brooks, as the impurities and disease are filtered out.

"I know the place...where he should rest eternally," Libby says through her tears.

They pick Leif's body up and carry it across the desert. A crack in the dried sand wide enough for them to fit through, but it isn't necessary. Sulien, in the change, earned the ability to portal. They lay Leif's body hidden in a cavern over the scythe of immortality. Unspoken words exchanged between them. None of them ever want the tool used again, ashamed of their actions. The ring made from the red Iolida flower rests on his finger. They leave it there.

His soul, long since escaping Leif's mortal body, wasn't harvested. Its fate is to

roam the middle realms and Kymani
understands well. It will always be unsettled,
and that is his own guilt and weight to bear.

"We will call it the desolate land and
warn our ancestors of its horror and sorrow,"
Sulien says as he gazes on Leif's lifeless body.
An emptiness growing in his soul. He will
never forgive himself for what they did…
What he did.

They choose new names for their new
life to erase their past, to ease their pain.
Libby names Sulien Drakal, meaning father of
the dead. He accepts that name, unaware of
its origin…unaware Leif was the true Drakal.
Kymani takes Delgon, meaning unharvested,
and Libby Alanni – survivor.

To hide their secrets and bury their
regret, Sulien modifies his scrolls, and they dig
and brick an area deep inside the earth. Above
it they build a fountain and, as their numbers
grow, a tower. Drakal spells the room with
strong magic, warlock in origin.

He gives Delgon the ascendant. It is
the reason Kymani was present that day. If it
wasn't for Sulien's need to bring back life
after death and his secret portalling, Kymani
wouldn't have been there. He'd still be a
hybrid harvester. Guilt, more guilt. He doesn't
want to see the ascendant again or remember
his former life. He doesn't ask what Kymani
will do with it.

Realm Walker

Drakal sends a message to Marcus in Thraves, using Alanni's new power of mind bending. He asks to meet at the falls during the day, so Marcus will be comfortable with the exchange.

They can't live in daylight. Like those he created, it burns their flesh. They heal quickly, but can't be exposed to the sun for long. Every creature has its weakness. Theirs is sunlight and lycan blood, but only Drakal and Delgon know of the second weakness. It's one they will keep quiet. The sunlight isn't one they can hide. The barriers of their red sky mark the boundaries of their survival.

Marcus stands under the falls in the cave. Carlan parts the curtain of blood with his pearl staff. His chestnut hair flows over his chest and his beard is neatly trimmed. His shoulders square and posture straight as a board. It is the first time Drakal has seen the man outside his office. He remembers the book and its ever present, always writing invisible hand of the dead. Are they in that book? Is Leif? He thinks not. It is a guide to the dead of the outer realms, not the middle.

Sulien carries the scythe that reverse-harvests. It is of no use, a worthless tool of his former life. Something that reminds them all of their remorse. A daily reminder of their transgressions. It is impossible to start new with the past staring them in the face. His grip around the smooth handle he labored over. A labor of desperation. "I'm ready to make the deal. A trade for this scythe."

Marcus doesn't flinch, his swirling eyes shifting from the driftwood head and meeting Drakal's. "Name your price."

"You will send us the dead from Lols who want a second life. You will give them the option." He doesn't say, but thinks, *if you renege on the deal we will go to Lols and take them.* The skills they gained through the change aren't something the harvesters, or any other subspecies, need to be privy too. The less they understand of the vampire way, the better for them. They must secure the survival of their subspecies.

"You have a deal." His eye falls to Delgon, as if searching for Kymani, or maybe missing his prized hybrid harvester. One who knows the outer realm well and cleaned up after the purebloods. That was his value, and now the lost souls will remain lost to wander Lols until another hybrid comes along with his unique abilities, maybe a descendant.

They build their family, their subspecies, with each new commoner – they decide. It makes what they do less humanizing, allowing them to believe they are truly doing good, helping the otherwise dead to live. To have a second life. Giving those without magic a special skillset.

How they transition the dead is not of harvester business but vampire. The process no longer needs a tool, but their blood. The blood of Leif running through their veins, pumping through their hearts. It is his sacrifice through them that makes it possible for vampires to live and make others. A single drop from one of them, and fresh blood from the vein of a commoner, to finish the transition. Their unique abilities allow them to travel, trap, and wipe the memories of those commoners.

Each one they make is their child. They are connected, feeling their emotions and thoughts.

Through the centuries, they continued their passage to Lols, extracting and returning commoners until magic veined across the land, stretching to all corners like Blood River. Its offshoots varying factions, one unknown to another. Like realms within a single realm. Hungry for the weak magic, commoners learned to spell items to amplify and began practicing blood sacrifice.

When the great sorceress arose Drakal, Alanni, and Delgon agreed to not return to Lols or give their children reason to return in fear their visits caused the imbalance. A community of willing commoners was built with the finest luxuries of the middle realms. By this time the outer and middle realms were divided, curtained off from one another.

The truth was eventually lost with time.

EPILOGUE

left Drakonia to never return. The small, wiggling bundle in my beak. I left him in Verboten with trolls who will raise him. He is ten now, and taking well to his magic. Not quite a troll nor an elf, or even a warlock, but something uniquely different. His magic strong, his adopted family hides him from the prying eyes of purebloods for fear. Hybrids with strong magic are a threat, unlike hybrids, like his mother, whose unique abilities were unknown or harmless. He is a strong child who doesn't know of his heritage, nor what he will sacrifice one day, along with his descendants.

The vampires stay in their realm, as the sunlight burns their flesh, and drink the red liquid of life from the falls. They have worked a deal with the harvesters, as Leif's death made it possible for them to bring life back from death. The community is small but growing. They have erected a large tower over a fountain of blood. They call it the ministers' tower and live there.

I, Sisimo, live in the treacherous lands with all other creatures who fit nowhere else. I am the only griffon. It is the place I call home, with the serpents, dark nymphs, pixies, and dryads.

The end of the Realm Walker Saga

Life after Death

Suggested Realm Walker reading order:

These reading orders are suggestions only. Try one out or find your own.

Enjoy the Ah Ha moments (order written by author)

To thoroughly enjoy the HFN

The prequels can also be read first and Life After Death last.

Acknowledgements

My gratitude and thanks to every reader who has enjoyed the Realm Walker series. It's been a long journey filled with tears, laughter and contemplation.

Many thanks to my editor, Dawn Lewis, who has been with me from the start. We have worked as a team through the ups and downs of many series and she has become a dear friend.

Thank you to every friend and family member who has supported my writing journey from the start until today.

Realm Walker started with a simple idea that led to a vast series. Nine books! I never imagined the series would go this far. Originally, I'd planned three books. It soon became four then I realized other characters and situations needed their stories.

Life after Death is the story that ties most of the series together. It's the beginning, long before Terra and Cyrus.

Thank you all very much!

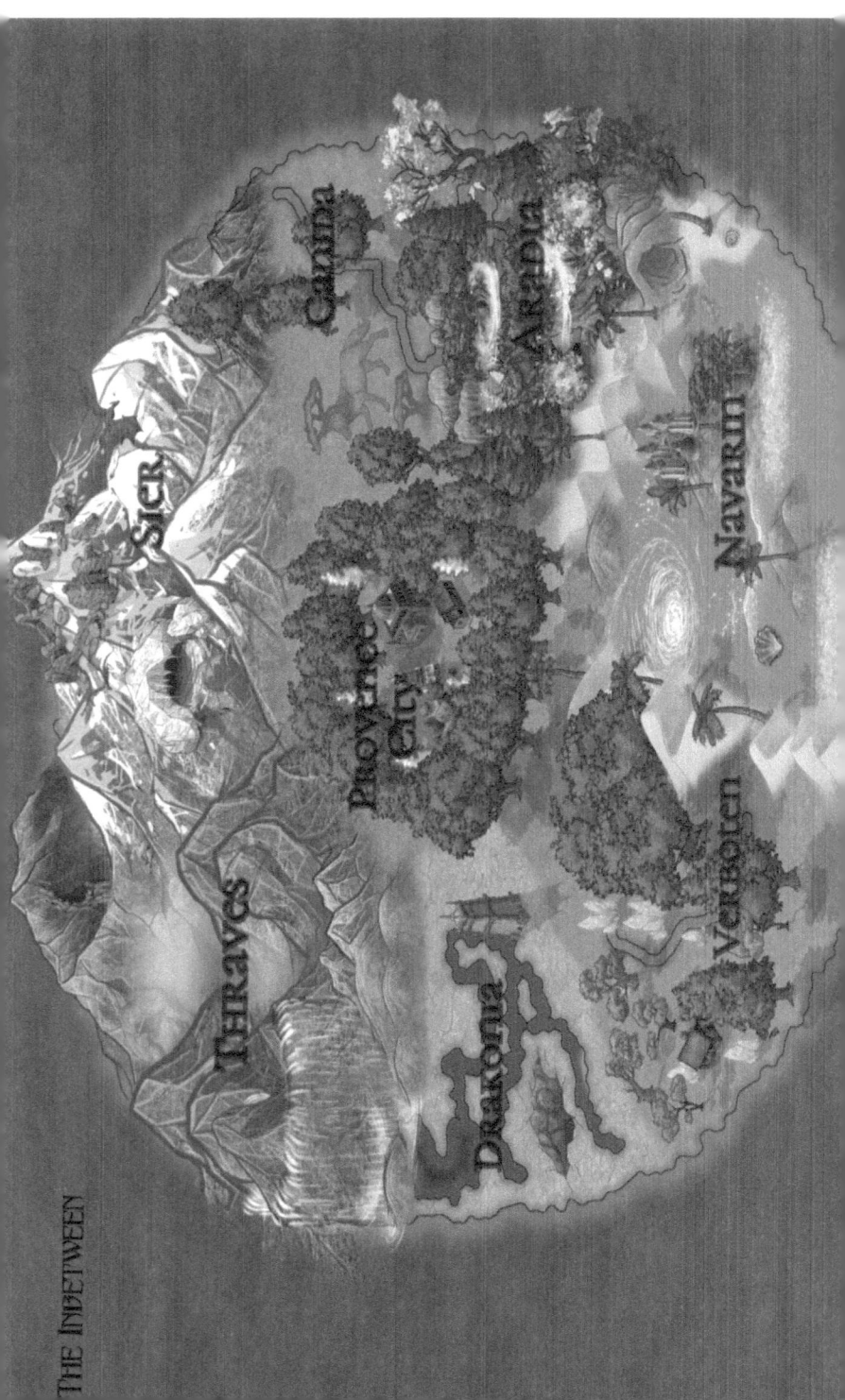

THE INBETWEEN

www.ingramcontent.com/pod-product-compliance
Lightning Source LLC
Chambersburg PA
CBHW030854200726
48289CB00003B/750